CLAIMED BY THE CYBORGS

INTERSTELLAR BRIDES® PROGRAM: THE
COLONY - 9

GRACE GOODWIN

GET A FREE BOOK!

FIND YOUR INTERSTELLAR MATCH!

YOUR mate is out there. Take the test today and discover your perfect match. Are you ready for a sexy alien mate (or two)?

VOLUNTEER NOW!
interstellarbridesprogram.com

1

Danika Gray, Interstellar Brides Processing Center, Miami, Florida

arm, strong hands held my naked body in place, the large, rough fingers wrapped around my hips from behind. Heat flooded me from the muscular chest pressed to my back. My legs were spread wide, wrapped over the male's thighs I sat on, my pussy open and on display.

My pulse raced, my flesh shivering in anticipation of...something.

"Do you accept my claim, mate? Do you give yourself freely, to me and my second, or do you wish to choose another primary male?"

Ummm, no? I wanted to tell this man, whoever he was, that I had no intention of accepting his claim on anything, but the body I seemed to be occupying shivered with need at the deep timbre of his voice, my—her—core throbbed, wet with welcome.

"Yes. Yes, I accept your claim, warriors." The voice wasn't mine, but I felt what she was feeling. Achy. Empty. Desperate.

Loved. Adored.

Safe.

That was *not* me. I had felt nothing similar in more years than I cared to count.

"Hurry," I—she—whispered.

From behind me, a second male voice murmured into my ear, "So greedy, little mate."

From somewhere around us a chorus of male voices spoke in unison, "May the gods witness and protect you."

I had no idea what was happening, but I knew the sound of promise in the male's voice. So did this body. A soft moan escaped from my throat as his hands moved from my hips to cup my breasts. He plucked and pulled at the sensitive nipples as I wrapped my ankles around his calves.

I sat on his lap. Content to be there.

Was that a massive cock pressing against my ass?

Oh God. Yes. It was.

I should have been shocked. Instead, raw lust flooded me, and I somehow knew there were two lovers. Two males. Both *mine*.

And this woman? This body? She was beyond greedy, comfortable and secure in their arms. She wanted both of them inside her, right now.

"Lift your arms above your head. Lean back. Wrap them around me and don't let go," that voice whispered in my ear again, the command one I was eager to follow.

I did as instructed, my breasts thrust forward, my back arched.

"Do not move without permission, mate."

A flicker of sass moved through the female body I occupied, but then she focused on the sound of male voices chanting all around us.

I tried to open my eyes, but the thought carried no weight as my body was not obeying *my* commands but *hers*. Whoever she was. She kept her eyes closed, and I knew it was because her primary male—whatever *that* meant—had ordered her not to open them and she wanted to please him. Wanted the pleasure she knew cooperation would award her.

Desperately.

"Do you accept me as your second, mate? Do you claim me as your own?"

"Yes. You are mine. Both mine. Hurry."

The first voice chuckled, much closer now, directly in front of my face. The hot brush of his laughter kissed my lips like a phantom. "Lift her nipples for me, second."

"In a moment. First I must fuck her ass, make her mine."

Wait. Wha—

The male beneath me shifted and used his strong hands to lift me by my hips. He settled me up and back against him until I felt the press of his hard cock at my tight entrance.

"Are you ready for me?"

No.

"Yes." I—she—responded, even wiggling my hips to take the tip of his cock inside.

It was his turn to groan as I used the hands I had tangled in his hair to pull him closer, rolling my hips in a small circle, taking him deeper, inch by inch.

His huge cock slid in easily, some type of tingling lube already inside my ass. With a pop he slid deep, both of us groaning. This body welcomed the sensation, knew it well. Expected more. Wanted more. Needed it.

My pussy fluttered and throbbed, empty.

The male in front of me sucked first one nipple, then the other into his mouth as my body clamped down on the hard cock filling me from behind. He suckled, rolled my nipples on his tongue. He tormented me with pleasure until even the voices faded and there was nothing but *them*. My mates.

Moving his way from breast to stomach, my primary male kissed me everywhere, his touch hot and lingering, taking his time as both my second and I waited, the anticipation growing until I felt like I was going to explode if he didn't fuck me soon. Fill my pussy with his hard cock. Pound into me with a relentless rhythm I needed.

Somehow I knew he was delaying, pushing me, making me wait. They were both in my mind, their emotions, their desire for me without limits.

I was everything to my mates. Life and death and even their air. They worshipped me, cherished me.

I felt love, hot and painful and unfamiliar, pour into my soul like molten lava, leaving a path of agony and bliss all in one.

Tears leaked from my eyes—her eyes? I didn't know

who was crying, but my mate's kiss gentled and he slipped a finger into my wet heat. "Are you ready for me, mate? Ready to be ours forever?"

"Please." This time when the female voice answered, I was in complete agreement. I wanted to scream, *Fuck me! Do it! Take me. I need to belong to someone...*

He worked me, fucking me with first one finger, then two. Three. When I was riding the razor's edge of release, he moved to kneel between my legs, still spread wide on my second mate's open lap.

He pushed his cock in slowly, the stretch forcing a keening wail from me—her—as he finally, *finally* filled me with his hard length, stretched me—her—to the limit with one mate buried balls-deep in my pussy, the other in my ass.

He pulled back once. Twice. Pushed deeper. Harder. Faster.

My second gasped at the friction, the pressure of my primary mate's cock rubbing my pussy walls, the thin barrier between them.

Their combined sensations, their pleasure poured into my mind. My body exploded, the orgasm ripping through me like a stick of dynamite had been lit inside my pussy, my entire body arching, reaching, needing...

"Miss Gray? Miss Gray? Can you hear me?"

Nooooo!

The chanting faded, the heat of my mates' touch, their scent. The emotions left as well, the fire of belonging that had burned so brightly completely gone, the aching pain of loving someone so much dissipated like fog under the brightness of day. Somehow the absence left me feeling even more alone, colder than I'd been before.

Now I knew what could be, what other people had, and I wished I had remained ignorant. I was used to the cold reality of my life. But my—no, *her*—mates had woken up a part of me I'd killed off long ago. The needy part. The *weak* part.

"Miss Gray? Please, nod if you can hear me."

The vision, or dream, faded completely, and I realized I was sitting in a not-so-soft chair, kind of like the one in the dentist's office, or maybe a rock-hard leather recliner. The amount of air I felt on my legs and feet reminded me that I wore something similar to a hospital gown.

The Interstellar Brides testing facility. Right. I was in Miami, Florida. Almost fifteen hundred miles from the small town in upstate New York that had once been my home.

'*Health, History and Horses.*' That was our small-town motto. Pathetic.

I never wanted to go back.

"Miss Gray?"

Reality refused to wait. I opened my eyes, irritated that my body still felt heavy and needy, my pussy wet, my nipples hard points beneath the gown. This sucked.

"I'm here." I tried to lift a hand to brush the hair out of my eye and was brought up short by the handcuff locking me to the processing chair.

Forgot about that for a few blissful moments as well. I was a criminal, after all.

"Excellent."

I turned my head and lifted my free hand to wipe the

offensive hair from my face. The woman speaking was called a warden—how fitting—and she was one of the people in charge of finding alien matches for human women and sending them off the planet. Which sounded like a damn fine idea to me. I had nothing here. Not anymore.

Before the dream thing, I had hoped to have freedom to live my own life. Nothing more.

Those two men had changed that. Now I was full of dreams. Hope.

I hated hope. Worst emotion ever invented. God's curse on the world. The ultimate carrot in front of the proverbial donkey...me. "Did it work? Because I've heard those computer dating apps never work." Truth be told, I hadn't really thought this would do much better.

"Oh yes. Your results are excellent. You have been matched to a male from Prillon Prime."

"Just one?" Was that disappointment in my voice? No. Couldn't be.

"Yes. You are matched to your primary male. He will choose your second mate, and they will claim you together."

"Oh." My heart skipped a beat, floating in my chest like a balloon filled with helium. I told it to calm the fuck down, but it didn't listen.

I'd been matched to one, but he would bring along a friend. Just like the dream.

I rubbed my thighs together, the aftershocks of my orgasm still making it nearly impossible for me to remain still. I wanted more. A lot more.

I hadn't paid all that much attention to the reading

material they'd handed out at the women's prison. I vaguely remembered reading something about the Prillon men—aliens—mates—mating in pairs and sharing their woman. Or man. Their mate, whoever that turned out to be. A threesome.

My mind went straight to the vision of three totally hot men getting it on, and I nearly groaned aloud, my eager pussy pulsing in agreement with my overactive imagination. What would I do with three?

Damn. Maybe I should have been matched to Viken. I read about that place, too. Three hot mates. Their cum did something to their mate's body to make them so horny they could barely think straight. At least, that's the idea I'd taken from reading one of the previous bride's personal accounts of being matched there.

No. *Shut up, Danika.* Sheesh. I did not *need* three mates. To be perfectly honest, I didn't even need one. But I *wanted.*

Maybe I'd just been in prison too long. If it hadn't been so damn true, I would have laughed at the thought. I was really, really tired of masturbating alone in my cell. I'd never been into women, much as I wished otherwise a couple times over the last few years. I'd tried. Couldn't get past the first kiss. Just not for me. I wanted what I wanted.

And I wanted cocks. Big chests. Deep, growling voices. Men that smelled like men. Dominant, muscled mates who would be big enough to protect me from every monster there was. I was so tired of fighting. So freaking tired of this planet and all of its bullshit.

"Miss Gray, did you have a question?" The warden was blinking at me, and I realized I'd been staring into space. Her bright blue eyes reminded me of the blue chewing gum that was my current favorite. Blue Mint Blast. Good gum. Really good. So strong it cleared my sinuses in about a minute flat.

"So, I get matched to one, but he gets to choose the other one? What if I don't like the second?"

"Do not worry. That is almost never an issue. Your mate will choose a male he deems worthy of you."

I didn't feel all that worthy of anyone at the moment, but I didn't offer her that information. This was about not going back to that hell-on-earth prison cell, nothing more.

"Now what?" I asked. This warden was young; if I had to guess, I would be surprised if she was thirty. But her pale blue eyes were kind, and her ivory skin was literally flawless. She had her dark brown hair styled into a bun, so I couldn't see much there, but she was beautiful. Add to that, she had an amazing French accent. So not fair. I wondered why she wasn't mated. Why work at a place like this when she could leave, get a hot alien mate, and go on her own adventure?

"Warden Egara? Can you come in now?" This young woman's name was embroidered on her maroon Interstellar Brides Program uniform. *Warden Bisset.* When she turned, I saw another woman step into the room. She appeared to be near the same age but with sad gray eyes.

"I observed Miss Gray's processing. You did an excellent job, although for the bride's comfort, I would suggest pulling the next candidate from the neural processors a few seconds earlier, nearer the beginning of her initial release."

Wait. What? No. However, even as I thought the protest, my body shifted on the exam chair, searching, in vain, for something to rub against. I had never been this turned on in my life.

"Of course, Warden Egara. Thank you."

The more experienced warden smiled kindly and then turned to look at me. "Warden Bisset has done an excellent job. Your match is ninety-nine percent. We see that with a very small percentage of our brides."

"Ninety-nine percent? What does that mean?"

"It means your mate will be absolutely *perfect* for you." Warden Bisset beamed, clasping her hands together in front of her face like a cheerleader rooting on her team.

Warden Egara was watching me with an intensity I recognized. She was not a woman who missed much. Her kind were dangerous on the inside, as if she'd ever been to prison.

Then again, who knew? I didn't know much of anything these days.

"Okay. Ninety-nine percent sounds good. Now what?"

Warden Egara turned to Warden Bisset with raised brows and an expectant look. "What now, Warden?"

"Oh! Sorry! Of course." Warden Bisset hurried to a table and lifted a tablet from the smooth surface. She carried it back to stand next to my bed as she read.

"Miss Gray, are you currently in a legal marriage or mating agreement recognized by any sovereign nation of Planet Earth or any other planet in the Interstellar Coalition of Planets?"

"What? No." I looked at Warden Egara, who was

nodding in approval. "These aren't the questions I read in the brochure." I had actually taken the time to read the legal questions and conditions required of potential brides. And this wasn't it.

"The prime has negotiated new terms for human brides based on requests from various warriors waiting for mates, particularly those on The Colony."

"What?"

She shook her head at me. "Just listen and answer the questions please."

Warden Bisset continued, "Upon execution of a bridal contract, do you attest that you are not leaving behind any children who are legally under your protection?"

"I don't have any children. But what if I did?"

She glanced up, her pale eyes serious. "The children would have been entered into the matching protocols. A legal document recognized by your court system would be required, stating that the bride has the right to relocate the child or children to another planet. But as you have no children, that is not an issue."

"Then why ask me again?"

"Protocol," Warden Egara answered. "The prime does not like mistakes that will affect his warriors. Therefore, we confirm your status multiple times."

"Okay. I do not have children, and I am not legally married to anyone. Anything else?"

"Do you attest that you are over the age of eighteen?"

"I'm twenty-three. You know that. I had to give you my birth certificate."

"Protocol, Miss Gray."

Bureaucracy. Rules.

Lies. I'd been through the foster system. The court system. The prison system. And now this. I was well past the age of believing anything these women were promising me.

I couldn't keep my mouth shut. One of my flaws. I had to challenge authority. "What if I was sixty?"

"Again, Prime Nial negotiated several changes to the usual bride protocols. The Interstellar Coalition of Planets has advanced medical equipment, and many warriors are more interested in a lover and companion than the age or child-bearing potential of a mate. As you stated you prefer to remain child-free, that preference has been entered into the system and you have been matched to a mate with similar preference."

"This is soooo not a dating app."

Warden Egara looked seriously offended, her scowl creating deep lines between her brows. "No, Miss Gray, it is not. We are responsible for matching our brides to the most honorable of all Coalition warriors and fighters. We do not make mistakes. They have suffered enough." Turning on her heel, she nodded to Warden Bisset. "Begin her processing. I have received confirmation that her mate is on The Colony." She looked at me. "Good luck, Miss Gray. As always, if you do not accept your mate and wish to be matched to another, your choice will be honored and you will be matched to another Prillon male."

Yeah, right. Like I believed that. But it didn't really matter. The money I'd received for being a bride was going to pay for my baby brother's college degree and leave him enough left over to put a down payment on a house. It was the only thing I could give him now. A chance at a normal life that had been stolen from me.

"You will have thirty days with your mates to make your final decision."

"And it's totally up to me? They can't just dump me and go after someone else?"

The warden looked truly shocked that I would even propose such an idea. "Oh no. You are his matched mate, the perfect female for him. Interstellar Brides are a great honor and a gift to the warriors and fighters who served in the war with the Hive. He would never willingly give you up."

Another thing I didn't believe, but there was no reason to argue. I was going out into space, to a new planet, regardless. "Okay, but I don't understand. When do I go? Is there a ship coming to pick me up?"

Warden Bisset clapped her hands twice, clearly excited about something. "I have been *dying* to get a chance to do this." She pressed her fingers to the tablet, and the wall next to my chair opened to reveal a large blue pool surrounded by soft lighting. It looked like the inside of an expensive spa.

"Just relax, Miss Gray."

My chair moved, sliding to the side, and I noticed the tracks on the floor would take me directly into the blue water, chair and all.

A few seconds later I was neck-deep in the warm, blue liquid, and a sense of contentment and relief filled me at once.

"That's it, Miss Gray. Relax. The NPU will be placed now. Hold still."

A strange robotic arm moved toward me, the tip touched my head directly behind my ear. A sharp burst of pain made me startle. "What was that?"

"Your neural processing unit. By the time you arrive on The Colony, the NPU will have integrated with the language centers of your brain and will help coordinate real-time language translation on every Coalition planet."

Wow. But, ow!

"That's the worst of it. Go to sleep. When you wake up, you will be on The Colony with your new mate."

"Now? Right now?"

"Of course."

"I'm not ready."

"You are. Your processing will begin in 3...2...1..."

The world went black.

2

Captain Varin Mordin, The Colony, Two Days Earlier

The stinging cold of transport faded, and I fell into a battle crouch.

"Clear the transport room! He's not in control!" I shouted the warning even as my oldest friend, Thomar Arcas, bellowed with battle rage and leaped toward the transport officer.

Thank the gods two Atlan guards stood between the Viken officer and the contaminated warrior. In this state Thomar would kill without a second thought.

"The transport origin station said he was sedated!" the Viken yelled as I struggled to hold Thomar back with both arms wrapped around his waist.

"He was! I warned them this would happen. They didn't fucking listen." Thomar was not in control. The collars we wore connected us, mind to mind, but with the chaos of our recent escape and multiple transports on

our way to The Colony, he was lost to his rage, memories
of our torture. He saw enemies everywhere.

The agony of his implants consumed him.

"Dr. Surnen to transport. Now!" One of the Atlans
yelled the command. I assumed some kind of comm
system would activate and relay the message. We needed
the doctor and enough sedative to take out ten Atlans.

Thomar fought me. Broke free.

"Thomar! Stop!" I tackled my friend before the two
Atlans had a chance to react. Thomar was in no condition
to be here, yet I'd refused to allow him to die, argued with
the medical officers on the battleship, convinced them to
give him a chance. Dr. Surnen was on The Colony. He
was the foremost expert on Hive integrations and their
removal. If anyone could save Thomar, it would be
Surnen and his medical team.

Perhaps I had made a mistake.

I grappled with my friend, keeping my mind calm as I
attempted to reach the part of him that was still Prillon,
still male. Still sane.

"Thomar, it's me, Varin. Stop fighting me!"

"Hive! I can hear them!" He shoved me off and to the
side, but I pulled him with me, rolling both of us off the
transport platform, down some steps, and onto the floor.
The two Atlans approached, but I held up my hand to
stop them.

"Don't! I won't be able to bring him out of it."

"We can handle him," one of the Atlans assured me.

"No, you can't. Trust me." I wasn't sure what they had
done to Thomar, not completely, but he could tear metal
walls down, rip ships into pieces with his bare hands, and

lift entire shuttle craft. He'd always been a powerful warrior. The Arcas family of Prillon Prime was infamous for a reason, their battle prowess the most well-known and the most feared.

The collar around my neck gave me an all too familiar glimpse into Thomar's state of mind. The collars were sacred to Prillon males, meant only to be shared with a mate once we claimed her. The Hive had other ideas. They had trapped Thomar and me in a cruel experiment from which there had been no escape. They'd used our mating collars against us, locked us mind-to-mind to discover how much we could endure, how much of our agony transferred to the other, how much stronger we were together. They'd taken our mating collars and turned them into weapons, implanted them beneath flesh and bone so there was no way we could remove them without bleeding to death.

I refused to choose death for us. And Thomar? He was too fucking strong and far too stubborn to die.

We'd lost count of the days, the nights. After our escape, we'd been picked up by a ReCon team and transferred to a medical ship. But even they could not help us. Our only hope was The Colony and Dr. Surnen, a Prillon famous in the Coalition for saving many contaminated warriors and fighters. Even a few Atlans. He was our last chance. Our only chance.

Thomar threw me off, shoving me straight up into the air so high that my back hit the ceiling of the transport room. "Damn it, Thomar!"

He was on his feet before I crashed back to the floor. I managed to land in a crouch, but the Atlans hadn't listened. They were in beast form, advancing on Thomar's position.

"Don't touch him! I'm warning you."

"I am a warlord. I fear no Prillon warrior." The Atlan who spoke was, indeed, massive. His uniform had the name Warlord Rezzer displayed on his chest.

"He is not a Prillon warrior. He is more."

Rezzer ignored me, stepping toward Thomar.

The two circled one another, and I stepped between them. "Stop. He *will* kill you."

"We shall see."

Thomar grabbed me from behind, and I turned, grappling with him, trying with every fiber of my being to stop the impending fight. I'd seen Atlans on the battlefield. I knew this Rezzer could tear an ordinary Prillon warrior in half with little effort. But Thomar was more machine than male. The Hive Integration Units had worked on both of us for more than two years. Every fucking day. I doubted the Atlan could defeat me in my current state, and Thomar had always been half a head taller and fucking ruthless in battle.

"Thomar Arcas, Son of Satmar, on your honor, Prillon, stand down!"

"I have no honor."

"Fuck that. Listen to me. Stop. Fighting." I calmed my voice and my mind, tried to connect to Thomar and bring his aggression down about a thousand levels.

"I hear them, Varin. They are inside that one. That beast." He snarled at Rezzer over my shoulder, but I didn't dare turn around to see what the idiot Atlan was doing.

"We are on The Colony. He has integrations like we do. Trust me."

"Lies." The chaos in his head threatened to overwhelm my control as the months of torment and pain flooded both of our minds like acid, burning away all reason, all connection to who we'd once been. There was no anchor in his mind, only the storm.

I felt him slipping from me, knew there was nothing I could do to stop him.

"Get out! He's losing control." I shoved his shoulders, held him back for precious seconds. "Get out now if you want to live!"

The Atlan, Rezzer, looked bored. "I am not concerned about your Prillon."

He was either an idiot or had more integrations and was much more powerful than I had first assumed.

The door slid open with a slight whooshing sound and two small children ran inside. They were squealing with laughter. Shocked, Thomar froze, and I dared looked back, over my shoulder. The children were, indeed, small, the tops of their heads barely reaching Rezzer's knees. That didn't stop them. They ran for him and jumped, one grabbing each leg.

"Papa! CJ took ball. Give it back." The small boy glared at his sister, who held the ball in the tiny hand wrapped around Rezzer's opposite thigh.

"Make ball. Essen. Duh."

"Mom say no!" the boy argued.

"Duh. Duh. Duh." The little girl, hair in a braid that ran down the back of her head and past her shoulders, chanted the offensive word at her brother. My NPU could not process the word, and I had no idea why it was considered offensive.

Nor did I know what an *essen* was.

Thomar stood frozen, equally confused, the sights and sounds of children something neither of us had heard in quite some time, since before we'd been taken by the Hive. Even on our battleship, we'd avoided the mated families' section of the ship. Their reaction to Thomar's presence was one we had learned to avoid.

Rezzer looked down at the two, who appeared to be twins, and scolded both. "CJ, give your brother back his ball. You know he can't use the S-Gen machine yet."

The little boy tilted his head back and forth, taunting his sister.

"No! RJ make ball. This one mine. He lose his."

Rezzer sighed. Deeply. "RJ, is that true? Is that your sister's ball?"

The little boy shrugged, and even I, who had very little experience with children, knew his sister spoke the truth.

"I will make you a new one later. You need to go find your mother."

Both children clung tighter and giggled. "No. Papa! Papa! Papa!" They chanted, both of their little heads bobbing enthusiastically as they finally agreed on something.

Frozen, shocked at the appearance of *children*, real living, breathing children, I had forgotten the danger behind me.

"Children?" Thomar's voice sounded astonished, and I hoped he would calm. Instead I felt the moment his mind went black with rage. "The Hive are processing children!" His bellow threatened to split my head in two.

"Get them out of here! Now!" I yelled at the Atlan, who had already taken a step back, the other Atlan stepping between me and Rezzer, who was carrying his startled children toward the door, both Atlans still in beast mode.

Why were they ignoring me? Why were they not panicked? Running for their lives? Were they idiots? Their lack of reaction made no sense. Thomar was dangerous. Deadly. A killer.

"Enough!" A Prillon wearing med-center green walked into the transport room and pointed an odd device in our direction. "I am Dr. Surnen."

I felt my shoulders drop in relief. Thank the gods. "Can you help us?"

"I will try." With that, he fired the strange device at Thomar, who slumped, unconscious, to the floor.

The relief I felt made me dizzy, my mind unable to cope with the sudden loss of connection to Thomar. We had been sharing emotions, sharing a mind for so long.

Wobbling, I turned to thank the doctor. I didn't have the opportunity as the doctor pointed the device at me and the world faded to quiet, blessed oblivion.

———

Thomar, Medical Station, The Colony, Two Days Later

I woke, the constant roar of Hive frequencies in my head present but bearable, lessened somehow. I blinked at the

lights over my head and turned my head to each side to
determine where I was.

Green stripes on the walls. Coalition Fleet insignia on
several pieces of equipment. A beautiful female—a
human—sat in front of an odd contraption with her eyes
pressed to two round openings. She appeared to be
looking at something inside the machine. The mating
collar around her neck was copper, and she seemed
serene. Unconcerned. Not in pain. Unafraid.

This was not the Hive Integration center.

I was in a medical station. A Coalition Fleet medical
station.

How was this possible?

"Where is Varin?" My voice rasped as if I'd been swal-
lowing sand for days.

She looked up at once, a bright smile on her face.
"You're awake! Thank God. I was worried that last treatment might do permanent dam—" She cut off the word
before finishing, but I knew. Damage. I was damaged
beyond all hope of recovery. I already knew that, even if
Varin refused to accept my fate.

"Varin?"

"He's in treatment right now. He should be back any
moment. He hasn't left your side. He's a worthy male, a
worthy second."

This human female did, indeed, understand our
ways, her assessment of Varin's honor correct. "Yes. He is."

"Your mate is so lucky to have you, Prince Arcas."

"Do not call me that."

"I'm sorry. It says here—" She indicated the small
tablet she was holding.

"Call me Thomar or Commander. And I am not mated."

She tilted her head to the side and walked slowly toward me where I remained restrained, multiple heavy straps holding me to the bed.

I could break them, easily, but I made no move to do so. She was small. Female. No threat. And she did not sing with Hive communications. Her body was not contaminated by their technology or mind control.

"Oh, but you do. She's on her way now. Dr. Surnen has been working nonstop the last two days to prepare you and Captain Mordin for her arrival."

"Impossible."

"She's your mate. Matched to you. You are her number one. Ninety-nine percent perfect match, big guy."

Big guy?

"Sorry. I'm Rachel. I'm mated to Governor Maxim Rone and Ryston. You're on The Colony now. In the medical station."

"How long?"

"Two days. Give or take a few hours."

"No. How long with the Hive?"

"Oh. I don't know. Just a moment." She walked to a display station and pulled my military record onto a large screen. I could see everything.

"Seven hundred forty-three days. Fuck." Red-hot rage filled me as I saw both the count and the bright warning beacon next to my name, the mark of dishonor, the mark used to punish and disgrace entire family bloodlines. Like mine. "I have no mate."

"She's arriving in transport within the hour. She's human. Like me."

"No."

"No? What do you mean no? You can't just send her back."

"Match her to another."

"Doesn't work that way. She has thirty days to accept or reject you, *Commander*."

"No. Send her back. Match her to another." I would not further dishonor my family by losing control and hurting a female. Never. I would not repeat my ancestor's mistakes. "I refuse the match."

"You don't have that right. You have to at least give her a chance."

"No. Where is Varin? I will speak to him now. I cannot accept a mate. I will not."

The tiny female walked toward me and dared place her small hand on my shoulder. She was either very brave or very stupid. The slight touch made me recoil. I was truly a monster, a creature the Hive had worked so hard to break. To create. To rule. No female of worth should lay a hand on me. If her mates were here, they would have every right to kill me for defiling her. "Do not touch me."

"Thomar, right? May I call you Thomar? Commander seems so boring and official."

"Yes."

"Earth girls are tough. Trust me. And the doc is very good at getting as many Hive implants out of warriors like you as he possibly can. You can have a life here. A happy life."

Such heartfelt and naive words. Truly females were the embodiment of hope for all warriors. But there was no reason for her to hold on to hope for me. "I can hear them, even now. The buzzing of the Hive collective fills my mind. They are everywhere and nowhere. I cannot control my thoughts. My actions. I am not capable of caring for a mate. I could lose control at any moment. Do you understand? I must not go near her."

In my mind, a blend of excitement and dread stirred. Neither emotion was mine. "Varin approaches."

"He does?"

No sooner had she spoken than my second, my oldest and most loyal friend, entered the medical station and walked to stand next to my bed. "Thomar. You are finally awake."

"I am. But I hear them still. Do you understand?"

Varin nodded. "I do." He looked across the bed and down at the small female standing next to me. "Lady Rone, we cannot accept a mate. You must contact the processing center on Earth and have the female matched to another."

Rachel stuttered as she glanced back at the screen where my image remained clearly visible. "I can't. I can't do that. It's too late."

Varin scowled and glanced at the screen. "Fuck. They have initiated final transport. She arrives shortly."

Rachel glanced from Varin to me. "Well, someone better go claim her or there is going to be World War III when the rest of the guys find out there's an unmated female up for grabs. And if I remember correctly, you Prillon warriors like them to arrive naked."

Varin groaned and our minds synced with the need to protect the unknown female. The unknown, naked female. "How many unmated males are on this base?" Varin asked.

Rachel grinned. "Hundreds. Better hurry." Was this Earth female enjoying our dilemma? Surely not.

"Go," I ordered. "Protect her until we can find another. Or claim her for yourself. Choose a second. Do not leave her unprotected."

"I cannot. We are bound."

"By the gods. I am sorry it is so."

"I am not." He looked at Rachel. "I will go to her and make sure no others challenge to claim an unprotected female. But Thomar speaks truth. We cannot claim her."

"As I told him, you don't have a choice. She will decide who keeps who."

Varin looked from the stubborn female to me. "Is this how she has spoken to you as well?"

"Yes." Indeed, I had never had a female be so...direct. Most warriors were terrified of me. Females generally avoided me at all costs—unless they wanted to bed a monster. After a while I'd taken what companionship I could get, knew it would never last. Hated myself for being weak.

Alone.

Varin shook his head to push my melancholy aside; I could feel the brush of his will inside my mind. We were one mind. Truly the Hive had succeeded in connecting us. My second scoffed and turned to face Lady Rone. "And this female is human? From your world?" Varin asked. "Will she be disrespectful and argumentative? Like you?"

I expected the female to protest. Instead, she burst into laughter. "I hope so."

Varin and I were one in our confusion.

Rachel walked to the display screen and pulled up an image I strained to see. The picture was of a female. Young. Beautiful. Long dark hair and solemn dark eyes. Her lips were full and ripe, and my cock hardened with need.

"Oh." Rachel's word was a quiet whisper of upset.

"What is wrong?" I demanded.

"She's a prison transport."

Varin growled. "The female was kept imprisoned on your world?" Our minds merged in shock and protective rage. "What barbaric place is this Earth?

"How long?" I asked.

"Are you sure you want to know? I mean, she's here now. It doesn't really—"

"How. Long."

Lady Rone cleared her throat. "Seven years, two months, seventeen days."

"Seven *years*?" Varin exploded, moving to the screen to see the data himself. "Your people placed her in a prison for seven years? Why? Why would you do something so evil?"

Rachel scrolled through some data, reading the Earthen language faster than either I or Varin could. We hadn't read text since before our capture, and now I felt the strain when I looked at the data. The Hive had broken more than my body. I felt ashamed. Ignorant.

"Let's see, at age seventeen—oh dear, she was a minor tried as an adult—"

"She was a *child*?" I fought for control, my rage at the mistreatment of this female, of any female, pushing me beyond my limits.

"Thomar. No." Varin closed his eyes and forced icy calm to enter my mind. Resolve to protect the female now. "We cannot change the past. She will not be harmed again."

Lady Rone was speaking softly, reading to herself. "She was convicted of..."

"Tell us. Now," Varin demanded.

"Murder. She was convicted of first-degree murder."

"What does this mean? 'First degree'?"

Rachel scrolled so that the female's face once more filled the screen, and I stared at the soft skin, shining hair. Now that I knew more about her, I easily recognized the look in her eyes for what it was. Despair. Grief. Loss of hope.

"First-degree murder means she planned it out before she did it. Premeditated. It wasn't an accident. It's the worst crime you can commit on Earth. She killed someone in cold blood."

Ice-cold fury settled in my gut, and I knew Varin shared my emotion as he turned to me with a scowl. "Only a female who was not protected would be forced to such an act."

"I don't know—" Rachel mused.

"Go. Protect her. She has suffered enough." I ordered Varin out of the room, and he left at once. Looking at Rachel, I studied her small, easily breakable bones, the delicate curves of her petite body. Human females were very, very small in comparison to the other races. Leaning back, I rested by head on the bed and closed my eyes. "Varin will protect her until she can claim another."

I heard Rachel's sigh. "We'll see. I was in jail, too, but not for murder." She sounded worried.

"Do not worry, female. You are mated. Your warriors would never allow anyone to hurt you."

Prillon warriors protected their females at all costs. Varin would protect the sad-eyed human until another could claim her. Or he would claim her for himself.

I needed to speak to the doctor. If there was any way to free Varin from the death sentence we currently shared, I intended to do so. I did not fear death. Varin deserved a mate, a life. Varin was a warrior of honor. Strength. He had kept me alive during our captivity. I would gift him back that life now. There had to be a way to break the connection between us, remove the collars the Hive had surgically implanted deep inside our spines.

"I need to speak to the doctor. Alone."

Lady Rone watched me, and the look in her eyes made me wonder if she knew what I had been thinking. She nodded and left me to stare at the image of the female staring down at me from the screen.

I would make the only honorable choice I had left.

I would set them both free.

3

Danika, The Colony

*N*aked? Really? Before I opened my eyes, the hum of a cold platform chilled my skin and rattled my bones. I was lying on my side. Good thing, because I was dizzy and felt like I was about to lose anything unlucky enough to be in my stomach.

Blinking slowly, I squinted at the lights until my eyes adjusted and I saw an alien, a freaking huge alien, kneeling next to me.

"Are you hurt?" His voice was deep and rough, like I imagined a giant would sound, with gravel in the back of his throat.

"I don't think so." I was about to complain about the whole naked thing, but he draped a soft black sheet over me. The fabric covered me from neck to toes with plenty of extra left over. Even better, it was thick, soft, and warm. "Thanks."

"My pleasure. It is my duty to care for you."

Alarm bells went off in my head, and I forced my eyes open to take stock of where I was and *who* I was with. He was massive, bigger than any professional athlete I'd ever seen in real life. I was tall for a woman on Earth, but he made me feel petite. His features were not human, his cheekbones sharper, the angles of his cheekbones and chin leaner and more defined. And his eyes. Gold rimmed with silver. Shimmering. Glowing. Like expensive jewelry.

"Are you my mate?" I asked.

Those glorious eyes closed slowly, as if he were in pain. "No. I was meant to be your second. I am Captain Varin Mordin. You may call me Varin."

"Danika." I sat up and wrapped the black fabric around me like a blanket as I studied him some more. He remained next to me, unmoving, allowing me to look my fill.

His skin was dark, no color I'd seen before but a dark, golden bronze. I reached out with one hand to touch the bared forearm and hand nearest me. They were covered in geometric designs, the color of the patterns matching the shining silver that rimmed his eyes.

He was strange. Exotic. Sexy as hell.

Memories flooded me from the testing dream, and I imagined that the male behind me, my second lover, had been him. His cock filling my ass. His deep voice pledging to care for me, protect me, love me. Forever. My second mate.

I'd never really imagined having two men in my life

before, but now that I had, I discovered the naughty little vixen in me wanted exactly that. Badly.

"Wait. Did you say '*was*'? What does that mean? If you are my second, where is my mate? The warden said he would be here—" I stopped before I said *to claim me.* My body knew what I'd been about to say. My breasts grew heavy, my pussy wet and eager for this alien, Varin, to shove me up against the wall and make me scream.

He sighed and stood, then reached a hand down to assist me to my feet. His touch was careful. Minimal. Not at all what I wanted. I wanted him to wrap his arms around me, pull me into his arms, and promise me everything was going to be okay.

But then, I'd never been that lucky.

"I will take you to speak to your matched mate, Thomar, as well as Dr. Surnen. They will explain things to you better than I."

"Doctor? I'm fine. I had a physical on Earth."

He released my hand and stepped back the moment I was steady on my feet. I missed the warmth at once and glanced at the lone male standing behind some kind of control panel. He looked human, if a bit on the large side. I had no idea what planet he was from, but I wasn't thrilled that a stranger I knew even less about than Varin was listening to every word and witness to the fact that Varin was rejecting me.

I knew it! I knew those wardens had been lying. Knew their stupid promises and that testing dream had been too good to be true. Damn it. I knew it.

So why were my eyes burning? My chest should not

feel like it was collapsing in on itself. I should have been prepared.

"Never get your hopes up, girl. Never. Don't forget again." I was speaking to myself, but Varin, the male here to reject me, apparently heard every word.

"You will be protected and cared for. I vow it is so."

I turned away from the humanish male running the control station and studied the wall behind Varin. What the hell was I supposed to do now? I did not believe him.

"I have confused you already."

I sighed and looked up at him—way up. "I'm not confused, just disappointed. I knew this was going to happen."

"What are you implying, female? Did they tell you Prillon males were without honor?"

"No. In fact, they told me how amazing this match was going to be. Ninety-nine percent. The warden told me my mate was going to be perfect for me. Perfect." I wiped the one stubborn tear from my cheek, irritated that I'd shown even that small weakness. "I'm just mad at myself for believing them."

"You accuse a warden of lying?"

Another tear. Damn it. "Just stating the facts. I'm here. He's not. And you have already told me he has no intention of claiming me. So, yes. Their promises were all lies."

Varin growled and stepped closer, his large hand cupping the side of my face with a strength and gentleness that made even more tears fall. What the hell was wrong with me? Well, other than transporting to another planet, naked, and being rejected by the sexiest alien I'd ever seen? Sure, mental toughness was important, but I was still human. Lonely. Tired of surviving on my own.

"I would give my life to protect you. I want you, more than you can comprehend."

"I don't understand. Then why?"

His thumb traced my bottom lip, and I leaned into his touch despite every intention not to. He was so big. So strong. And the way he was looking at me made me want to believe him. So badly.

"My lady, you are more beautiful than I imagined. Perfect."

"I don't understand any of this." He'd called me perfect? Beautiful? I was average looking, not ugly but nothing special. My nose was too big, my lips too thin. My eyes were plain. Brown. There was nothing spectacular or special about me. Maybe that's why he was doing this. Maybe aliens were typical men who wanted huge breasts, a tiny waist, and a woman who'd had lip injections and butt implants.

"Please, the doctor will explain Thomar's condition. Then you will understand why we cannot claim you." He removed his hand from my face, and I felt bereft.

"What condition?" I did not like the sound of this. Varin was sexy. Respectful. Strong. No one would mess with me with someone his size around.

Or...that's what I thought until a door slid open and a true giant walked into the room. I recognized his race from watching the *Bachelor Beast* television show back on Earth. He was an Atlan. And he was in full beast mode. "Maxim sent me. Varin?"

"I'm fine. I was just about to escort the lady to medical."

"Lady Arcas?" His voice was like the rumble of a rusted engine being forced to grind its gears after a long winter.

"She's not—" Varin began.

"I'm fine," I interrupted. That wasn't my name, but since I was the only woman in the room with three aliens, I assumed the Atlan beast was speaking to me. And I did feel well. Nothing hurt. I wasn't hungry or freezing cold, like I'd spent nearly every day of the last seven plus years. Physically I was tip-top, but mentally? This we-can't-claim-you routine was making me very nervous. I could not go back to that rank prison cell and rot for the rest of my life. I wouldn't. And the bride center had said I would have thirty days to decide what I wanted to do.

Didn't that mean I had thirty days? Even if I knew my mate, Thomar, didn't intend to claim me? I could at least relax for a bit, right? Get my own room? Soak in a hot bath and sleep without being worried about who or what might come at me in the dead of night.

Did it matter if they claimed me or not? I'd rather be dead than go back to prison.

Resolved stiffened my spine, and I stepped back to put a bit of distance between me and temptation. If I had thirty days, I fully intended to use every single one of them.

The Atlan grunted and turned back to face the door. "Come."

"My lady," Varin held out his hand, not to touch me

but to point toward the exit. "Please follow Warlord Rezzer. I will stay close to make sure no one thinks to challenge for you."

"Challenge for me?"

"No mating collar," Rezzer grumbled. "Dangerous."

"We didn't ask for your help or your opinion, Warlord," Varin's voice made me jump as I realized he was literally on my heels, his hot breath moving the hair on the side of my neck when he spoke. A shiver of desire ran down my spine. I ignored it.

"Prillon. Fools." The beast did not mince words.

Varin didn't bother to respond to the insult.

I followed the Atlan through a series of corridors of various colors until we reached an area where the walls were striped with green. Rezzer stopped in front of a door, waved his hand over a panel to open it, and stepped to the side like a palace guard stationed outside a throne room.

Obviously he expected me to walk inside. So I did, stepping into a large area with softer lighting and four people wearing green moving here and there, from bedside monitor to microscope to touch screen and back. A large male with features similar to Varin's looked up when I entered and immediately walked to intercept me. His uniform was a darker green color than the others. Like Varin, he was huge, his face angular. Alien.

"Welcome, my lady. I am Dr. Surnen. My mate, Mikki, is also from Earth."

I looked closer and noticed the steel-gray collar partially hidden by his green tunic. So he had a mate from Earth? That was interesting. So there were other Earth girls here? How many? That might be fun. Hopefully they weren't mean. I was tired of mean people.

"Nice to meet you, Doctor. I'm Danika Gray." I held out my right hand, and he took it, proving he had some familiarity with human customs. I noticed that his left hand, which held some kind of tablet, was streaked with silver.

"Of course." He smiled as he gently squeezed my hand. The stretching of his golden facial features somehow made him look more alien rather than less. He was like a lion, golden from head to toe. His eyes, however, were totally alien and reminded me of the frozen lemonade popsicles I used to share with my dad on our front porch on hot summer days.

"You are Danika Gray from Earth, matched to Prillon Commander Thomar Arcas with a ninety-nine percent compatibility score. Quite remarkable."

"She is," Varin confirmed before I could speak. I released the doctor's hand and pulled the black fabric more tightly around myself. Awkward. I was barefoot and wearing nothing more than a sheet while talking to aliens on another planet. My life grew stranger by the minute.

"Please, Danika, come with me. I will do my best to explain." Dr. Surnen's tone was relaxed, and his unperturbed expression did more to calm me than anything so far.

I walked along behind the doctor toward the back section of the medical area where a door opened to reveal what reminded me of a standard hospital room back home. The alien on the table appeared to be unconscious or deeply asleep. His face was turned away from me, but I could see just enough to determine that his eyes were closed. He was bare-chested but covered from his shoulders down by a green sheet. However, the thin fabric did nothing to hide his gigantic body. He was even bigger than Varin. Maybe as big as the beast, Rezzer. Bulging muscles. More of those strange silver geometric designs on his shoulders and neck. He looked fierce. Monstrous. I shivered as my nerves went into overdrive and my pussy throbbed.

He scared me, and that made me wet. Hot. Desperate to touch him. Trace the marks on his flesh. Kiss them. Taste his skin. Ride his cock.

He was mine?

Holy shit.

The three of us walked inside the room, and the door slid closed behind us. A series of quiet beeps and signals filled the tranquil space, reinforcing the feeling of being in a hospital with patients hooked up to gadgets and monitors.

I stepped closer, wanting to see my mate's entire face.

Dark brown hair, skin the color of tanned leather. His features were sharper than a human man's, just like Varin's and the doctor's. His eyes were closed, and I wondered what color they were. Varin's were gold and silver, but the doctor's were yellow. Another Prillon male I'd seen outside this room had warm brown eyes similar to a human's.

Something inside ached to have him open those eyes

and look at me. See me. Want me. Me! Danika Gray. Orphan. Criminal. Lost soul.

"What's wrong with him?" I asked.

Varin stiffened where he stood next to me, his entire body drawn up tight, a scowl forming on his face. Deep lines appeared at the corners of his eyes, and I realized he was in pain. Physical pain. Judging by the change in his coloring—he looked a bit paler—I had to assume he was in agony.

The doctor walked to the side of Thomar's bed, and I trailed behind, eager to get a closer look at my mate's face. He was stunning to look at. I studied his full lips, imagined his kiss, his voice vowing to make me his forever. Varin behind me, vowing the same. Both of them taking me, filling me up, touching me. Kissing me. Making me come.

I wanted what I'd experienced in the testing protocols. How dare they tell me no?

Inspecting him, I noticed the large bulge beneath the sheet where his cock rested against his thigh.

That was big too. Shit. Was it hot in here?

"Well? Spill. What's wrong with him? Why is no one telling me what the hell is going on?" I needed the vision I had in my head. I needed to belong somewhere. This place, this unconscious Prillon warrior was my last hope.

"Doctor. Please," Varin insisted.

"I do not agree with his decision," the doctor said.

"It's not your place."

"Very well."

"What decision?" I asked, feeling like a child standing between two arguing adults. I really, really wanted to stomp my foot and scream at both of them. "He's my matched mate. Tell me. Now."

The doctor looked from Varin to me and sighed. Again. "Thomar has decided to sever his connection to Varin."

"What does that mean?"

"It means he's going to die."

4

Danika

"**W**hat?"

The doctor met my gaze, unflinching. "When I remove the collar linking their minds, Thomar will not survive the procedure."

"No. Get out," I ordered. This idiot was not touching my mate.

Neither male moved.

I pointed at Varin. "You. Stay." Then turned to the doctor. "You, get out. Now."

"My lady?"

"Get. Out!" This was *not* happening. My mate was not going to die unless he had a damn good reason. Nothing I'd heard so far convinced me that was the case. Was it stupid to be so attached to someone I had yet to meet? Probably. But he was more than a person. He represented so much more. A future. Belonging. Love. Hope. So much hope.

He was huge. Strong. So was Varin. Between the two of them I wouldn't have to fight every second of every day. I would be safe. Protected.

Both things I had not felt since I was eight years old. Since my dad died.

I didn't want to spend the next thirty days alone, locked up in a bedroom somewhere. I could. I would survive. But that was not what I wanted. I wanted the dream. No one was killing my hope, not when I'd had to fight like a demon to convince myself to feel it in the first place.

A human yo-yo, that's what I was. My head and my heart battling it out like two rabid dogs tearing each other to pieces. Every bite hurt, on both sides. One minute I was determined to turn away and make it on my own, the next I wanted to curl into my mates' arms and let them take care of me.

The doctor looked at Varin, who nodded slightly to indicate the doctor could leave. The small gesture made me even angrier.

"*Get out!*" I yelled.

The door opened and the doctor exited. Looking through the doorway, I saw the surprised and curious faces of the medical team before the door slid closed again.

"Does that lock?" I asked.

"Yes."

"Lock it."

"My lady?"

"I'm not your lady. I'm not your mate. Remember. You don't want me."

"That is not—"

"Just lock the door, please. I don't want anyone coming in here until I'm good and ready."

Varin studied me intently. I stared back.

"You are, indeed, very similar to Lady Rone."

"What does that mean?"

"Nothing of import. I will close the door." He walked to the door, his large frame blocking my view, but I decided to trust that he had done what I asked. When he turned back to face me, he looked confused. "What do you intend to do?"

"Change his mind."

"Impossible. I have tried."

I smiled and pulled the sheet down to reveal my mate's entire body. Thank all that was holy, he was naked beneath. Very naked. Huge chest, massive thighs, cock so big I knew I'd never be able to wrap one hand around it. He was secured to the table, held down like a prisoner by multiple, heavy straps across his chest, stomach and thighs. The strange geometric designs Varin had also covered Thomar's entire body, denser on his chest and neck, less so on his abdomen, nearly covering him from the hips down. I traced one on his shoulder with my fingertip. "What are these?"

Varin stepped forward, his gaze locked on my movement like a laser. "We were captured by the Hive. Those are biosynthetic integration nodules they placed in our bodies."

"But what are they?"

"Contamination. Dishonor. Torture."

I froze, the marks taking on a much more sinister meaning. I leaned forward and kissed one of the marks on Thomar's chest. When I lifted my gaze, it was to find Varin had stepped closer, the bulge of his hard cock clearly visible in his uniform pants. I reached out slowly and took his hand, raised it to my lips, and kissed a similar mark on his wrist. "I think they're beautiful." And they were. Scars. That's what they were. Proof that my mates were survivors. Tough. Resilient. Fighters. Like me.

I had some scars of my own, and I hoped they would feel the same.

Varin stopped breathing as my lips lingered on his skin. Maybe he did want me after all.

"What did the doctor mean when he said your minds are linked?" I asked, looking up at him through my lashes.

Varin pulled his hand from mine and took a step back as if I'd splashed him with a bucket of ice water. From a pocket he pulled a thin black ribbon and held it up for me to see. "They used collars just like this. The Hive forced us to create an unnatural bond using Thomar's mating collars. We hear each other's thoughts. Feel each other's pain."

I studied the innocent looking ribbon of black. Remembered Rezzer's words about me not wearing a collar. "Was that supposed to be mine?"

"We will never ask you to wear it."

"So the Hive bonded you and Varin. Mentally. Like mates?"

"Yes. But we had no mate to balance our aggression,

to soothe us or to feel pleasure at our touch. The Hive experimented on us, used the collars to determine if we would be able to endure more pain, accept more integrations than we could survive on our own."

"And did you?"

"Unfortunately. Our minds grew together until it became difficult to separate his thoughts from mine. We feel everything as one, see through two sets of eyes. Their experiment was successful. We are not able to separate our minds."

I looked at Varin's neck, only now realizing he did not wear a collar. I looked at Thomar's unmoving form. He, too, wore no collar. "I don't see any collars."

"They imbedded them along our spines, integrated them with our nerves and brain tissue. They cannot be removed."

I glanced down at Thomar and ran my hand over his arm, savored the heat of him, the strength I could feel just below the surface of his hot skin. "So he asked the doctor to kill him so your minds wouldn't be linked anymore?"

"Yes."

"Why?"

Varin was silent so long I forced my gaze from Thomar's face to look at my second.

"Varin? Please. Tell me." I used my softest tone, the voice I'd used to comfort my little brother on the worst nights when we hid in the closet and prayed for morning.

"He is in constant agony, and he cannot make it stop; the doctor cannot cure him. There is no physical ailment causing his pain, only the integrations."

"And you feel what he feels? Everything?"

"I do."

Now I began to understand. The lines of pain around Varin's eyes. The despair in his gaze. The lack of hope. I knew that look well. I'd seen it in the mirror thousands of times.

"Can he feel what you feel?"

"Yes. But it takes extreme emotion or pain for me to reach him. His torment is nearly impenetrable. The Hive tested his limits, desired to test their methods on his royal blood."

Royal blood? What did that even mean? Was my NPU thing translating correctly? Prillon Prime didn't have a king, they had a prime and he was mated to a human named Jessica. Everyone knew that. Even the out-of-touch humans on Earth knew that one of their own had gone into space and become a queen.

Or were there two queens? Two. Definitely two.

Whatever. Did I care if he was some kind of alien prince?

Nope. I had zero shits to give in that department. If my stepfather had taught me anything, it was that being famous did not mean you were a decent human being. I did not care about royalty or fame or money. I cared that he was mine, and I was not giving him up without a fight.

I lifted my hand from Thomar's arm and covered him once more with the sheet. Varin watched me but did not move, not even when I walked to stand directly before him, my breasts pressed to his body. I looked from his face down to the collar he still held in his hand. "I need to understand, Varin. I need to feel what you feel."

"No. It will cause you extreme pain. I am a male of honor. I will not ask you to suffer."

"I'm not asking for permission." I pulled the innocuous looking black ribbon from his hand and held his gaze as I did so. He could have stopped me, yet he chose not to. He wanted this, too. I stepped back, just a bit. Placed the collar across my palms. Studied it. "This is too big for any human to wear. Way too big." I figured it would go around my neck twice, or close to it.

"The collar's size adjusts automatically once placed." His voice cracked, and I noticed his hand shook. Was he frightened? In pain? I wanted to know. I needed to know.

I held his gaze as I lifted both ends of the collar up toward my neck. "Varin?"

"Yes, my lady?"

"I'm not going to choose another mate. I'm keeping Thomar. I'm keeping you, too. You are my second. Do you understand?" The ends of the collar touched behind my neck, and I released them as they moved of their own accord, shrinking to encircle my throat, heating against my skin. It felt like melted butter was sinking into my flesh.

"I should not allow you to do this."

"But you will. Because you want to save him, too."

"He is the most honorable warrior I know. He deserves a mate. He has suffered more than most could endure."

"Then let's save him together."

"How? I have tried everything to reach him. To relieve his pain."

I smiled even as my mind began to fill with pain that

rivalled an instant migraine. I ignored it, knew it wasn't my pain but a mere fraction of Thomar's. Of Varin's. Now it was mine, too, the collars linking the three of us together as we should be, as mates.

Yes, it hurt. I knew somehow that they suffered much worse, that they were protecting me from the worst of it, even now. I took a moment to breathe through it, make peace with the pounding inside my skull. Accept the pain as part of myself.

So what if I had a headache? If my muscles began to burn and tingle? If my bones ached as if they had steel levers trying to bend them from the inside. I'd been in pain before. Many, many times. I knew how to ignore it. How to use it.

Closing the distance between us, I pressed my body to Varin's heat. I dropped the black sheet to the floor to stand before him naked. Smiling in invitation, I found his hard cock with one hand and then squeezed him through the uniform pants.

"Have you tried fucking your mate?"

"By the gods, female, you do not know what you ask. I will not be gentle."

"I don't care. Fuck me. Fill me up. Make me come. Feel me around you." I squeezed his hard length, rubbed the tip with my thumb. "Touch me. Feel something good for once. Maybe that will change his mind."

Thomar groaned and I knew I was going to get at least one hard cock stretching me open, making me writhe and moan and ache. Since the moment I'd been in that testing chair, my body had developed a mind of its own. The greedy bitch wanted both of them, but for now Varin would be enough.

"Danika." Varin leaned down, his lips hovering above mine. His hot breath fanned my cheeks, and I realized his eyes were even more stunning, more beautiful than I'd realized.

My name coming from his lips made my heart ache in my chest. No one had ever said my name like that, like he longed for me, would suffer and die if he didn't touch me.

"Kiss me."

"There will be no turning back. I will never let you go."

What he meant as a warning soothed an empty place in my soul, anchored a part of my heart that had been drifting for a very long time. "Varin." Pushing up on my tiptoes, I kissed him gently. "Take off your clothes."

Varin did as I asked, stripping quickly as I watched. He was magnificent. Dark. Muscled. His body was covered in a patchwork of the geometric silver symbols, perhaps half as many as Thomar carried. He straightened to his full height, his huge cock hard and straining to reach me.

My pussy clenched around empty space, and I squeezed my thighs together in an effort to find some relief. "Varin." I didn't recognize the husky sound of my voice, the need, the pure raw lust taking over my body. I did nothing to lessen the need, hoping Varin would sense what I desired through the collars.

Moving quickly, Varin stepped forward and lifted me into his arms, my thighs coming to rest on his forearms. We collided as he claimed my mouth in a kiss that curled my toes, had my fingers digging into his hair. I wrapped my legs around his hips and wiggled, searching for his cock, wanting him inside me. *Now.* It was as if I'd been overheated from hours of foreplay since the moment I'd taken that damn matching test.

I was in pain—their pain. And I burned for them. For Varin. For the vision I'd had in that testing chair. The combination overloaded my system, all thought gone. I was a thing. A greedy, hungry, lustful creature, the pain I felt blending with need. Desperate. Ravenous. Impatient.

The collars worked some kind of magic. It was like I could *feel* my fingers pressing into my own shoulders, knew the pleasure Varin experienced at my touch. His mind was a whirling chaos of agony from both Thomar and his own engorged cock, the two merging into one overpowering need to fuck me. Find release.

His entire body shook as he fought for control.

I soothed him with my hands in his hair, stroked his neck and shoulders softly. Gently. "Can you feel me? How much I need you inside me?" My pussy hurt, the outer lips swollen and heavy, my entire body touch starved and hungry for him. The pain in my limbs pushed me to a place I didn't recognize, my entire body on the razor's edge, every nerve awake and screaming in bliss, in pain, with the need for release from both.

Without speaking a word he pressed my back to the wall, moved me exactly where he wanted me, and thrust deep. Hard.

I cried out at the invasion as he stretched me wide, filled me up. It had been so long. So very long and I'd not been with many men before—

No. I was not going to think about that. Not now.

The pain merged into something heated until there was nothing but pleasure. Passion. The scent of us together. The sound of his ragged breathing as he pumped into me in a relentless rhythm that had me gasping for air. Fighting to breathe. To hold on to him.

The orgasm hit me without warning, and Varin fucked me through it, drawing out my pleasure as I moaned and clawed at his shoulders.

Varin

This was wrong. And I could not stop.

Danika's hot, wet pussy clamped down on my cock and pulsed with her orgasm, her small hands pulling and scratching me with her need, her demand for more.

I lifted her a bit, adjusted her so I could move deeper inside her. My body took over, rutting into her like an animal I had no hope of controlling.

"Mine. Mine. Fucking mine." Fuck. I shouldn't have said that. Didn't care. I'd told her I would never give her up. I meant it. No matter what happened with Thomar, she was mine. My mate. I didn't give a fuck who I had to kill or what laws I had to break to keep her. Her scent was in my mind, the softness of her skin branded into my memory, the heat of her pussy, her cries of pleasure things I would never be able to give up or forget.

"Varin?" Thomar's voice called to me from a distance.

I ignored him, too lost in the pleasure of Danika's submissive body to respond. I could only feel. Need. Rut.

Danika came again, her soft cries turning into a quiet, keening sound that made my balls draw up tight. They ached and I knew I was about to fill Danika with my seed.

Which was Thomar's right.

No. We had agreed. No children. There was no breeding agreement. Nothing to stop me from—

"Varin?"

White-hot needles, thousands of them, pierced my flesh. A vise squeezed my mind, the agony Thomar carried with him driving into me as he woke from the sedative the doctor had given him.

"Ahhh!" Danika cried out with the pain, and I pressed deep, held her in place, and lifted one hand to cup her cheek. I stroked the soft flesh with my thumb until she opened her beautiful brown eyes and met my gaze.

"Stay with me. Here." I tilted my hips just right and she groaned. "Right here."

"Varin."

The pain faded to a dull roar, a background noise I could ignore, and I lowered my head, bent to kiss my mate with my cock still buried deeply inside her. "You're mine."

"Yes."

"Varin!" Thomar was fully awake now. I could feel the bed beneath him, knew he struggled to make sense of the scene before him. From his angle it must look like I was fucking the wall. I felt a bit of laughter bubble through my chest.

Shocked at the sensation, I kissed Danika harder.

Deeper. Tasted her mouth, explored her, claimed her, made fucking sure she would never get the taste of me off her lips.

She was a miracle. A fucking miracle. And she was mine.

I allowed the possessive thought to fill me up until it was the only thing I had in my mind as I pumped into her body, fucked her hard and fast and deep. I knew Thomar watched now, knew he hungered for her, craved to feel our mate on his cock, feel her soft skin beneath his fingertips.

His desire must have hit Danika as well, for she gasped and pulled her lips from mine, her neck arching as she tilted her head back and wailed as a hard orgasm rocked through her.

She took me with her, my cock pumping in and out of her as my seed filled her pussy. I'd marked her with my cum. The most primitive part of me wanted to rub her down with my scent, make sure no other male would ever touch her.

"Mine."

Danika looked up at me, her gaze serious. Solemn. Sated. "You're mine now."

I leaned down and pressed my forehead to hers, my chest burning with something I'd never felt before. I didn't argue. I was hers. I would do whatever I had to do to protect her, from myself, from the outside world, and from Thomar, whose angry voice filled the small room.

"What the fuck do you think you're doing?"

5

Thomar

The smell of wet pussy and seed filled the room. The female was here, her mind somehow linked to my own, her orgasm waking me from a deep, restful slumber.

There was only one possible way my mind could be linked to the female's; Varin had placed our mating collar around her neck. Placed her under our protection.

His naked ass moved plenty as I watched him from behind. I knew he was fucking a female, our mate, a human I had yet to see. His possessive and loyal nature already clouded his judgment. His lust and obsession filled my mind until it was hard to separate my thoughts from his, from the female's. Her emotions surged through my mind as well. Desire. Hunger. Longing. Fear.

She rode his cock, the burning pain of his rough thrusts driving her to the edge again, her body desperate for release, for another explosion of pleasure to overcome her anxiety. Insecurity.

Despair.

How could she feel so much pleasure and so much fucking anguish at the same time?

Varin had to feel her emotions as well. Or perhaps his desperate need to feel anything other than tortured had overcome his ability to reason.

Perhaps he had finally broken under the weight of our linked minds.

I groaned softly as I felt his release building, my own cock hard and eager to fill the hot, wet pussy he had already claimed.

He intended to keep her. Which would be honorable and right. But not with my mind, my constant torment linked to her as well. I would not allow any female to suffer when it was within my power to spare her. Especially my mate.

I could not formally claim her, but I could protect her, had made my wishes clear to both Varin and Dr. Surnen. The mating collar imbedded in my spine was to be removed, regardless of what happened to me. I would not be responsible for any more suffering. I could not. Not only had the doctor not performed the surgery to remove my collar, but Varin had given our female a mating collar and fucked her into oblivion within a few steps of my death bed?

"What the fuck do you think you're doing?" I growled at Varin, hoping the quieter tone would not frighten the female. They appeared not to have heard me, his thrusting hips slowing now that he'd filled her with his seed, found relief. She moaned with each tiny movement, very small hands clinging to his shoulders as he kissed her over and over, tasting what was mine.

How could any female have hands so small? So delicate?

She was our mate. *My* fucking matched mate. Bad enough I had to give her up. I would have much preferred not to see her first. Smell her pussy. Hear her soft, very feminine cries of need.

Feel the longing and vulnerability in her mind. She was lost. Needed protection. Everything honorable in me demanded I provide for her, yet I was unable to do so, the failure gnawing away at my sanity that much more as Varin sated her. Filled her up, their combined pleasure roaring through my mind like shock waves.

By the gods, she felt good. So hot. So tight. So fucking wet. Varin's obsession became my own. I would keep her. Fuck her. Protect her. Taste her. Fill her. Feed her. Bathe her...

"Varin. Stop. By the gods, you must stop." I could not endure such hope, such obsession.

Shock came from Varin through the collars as he registered my command.

From the female mind? Ripples of pleasure mixed with anxiety. Determination. She thought she could change me. Convince me to change my mind about my fate.

She was wrong. They were both wrong.

Small feet slid down from the sides of Varin's hips, along his thighs, and lower until they came to rest on the floor. Moments later a small female emerged from behind him. A small, very naked female. She walked toward me where I remained strapped to the bed.

My cock jumped at the sight of her full breasts and curved hips, a bit of precum leaking from the tip. Her skin was smooth and looked soft to touch. Her dark hair hung low, past her shoulders to frame her breasts. Her lips were full and ripe, her brown eyes glazed with passion. She looked exactly as a well-fucked female should.

I bit back a growl.

Mine. Fuck. She should have been mine.

"Hi. I'm Danika. You're mate."

"You are not my mate." I glared at Varin, who had turned around to face me. His gaze locked with mine, unrepentant. "I thought I made that clear."

Her mussed dark hair and graceful movement drew my attention. I should have continued to glower at Varin but could not take my eyes off the naked female. The blush of desire had darkened the flesh above her breasts. The seed sliding down her inner thighs had me clenching my fists in barely suppressed rage. My cock expanded, grew hard, hot, and painfully engorged. My entire body hummed with the need to carry her to the bed, lay her down, and fuck her until she forgot all about Varin, until the only name she could utter was mine.

Mine.

She was mine.

No.

Fuck.

"You should not be here, female."

"The name is Danika. And that's not your decision to

make." Her voice was soft, gentle, but I did not mistake her tone for submission. Could not with her desperation pushing into my mind.

"I do not accept the match, female. Leave me."

"No." Hands on her hips, she tilted her head and looked me up and down like I was a misbehaving child. "I don't have to choose someone else for thirty days. You're mine for thirty days whether you like it or not."

"No. I am not." I sat up slowly. The snapping sounds the straps made as they broke over my chest and thighs was a mere nuisance. The restraints had been more of a reminder not to give in to the white-hot rage burning through me every moment of every day than to hold me down. Dr. Surnen had counted on the sedatives to keep me quiet.

If Varin had not fucked her into orgasm, if their mutual pleasure had not flooded my mind, the sedatives would have been enough.

Now I was awake. My cock hard. And the female responsible stood before me naked, hand on her hip, giving me sass.

I slid my legs over the side of the medical bed and stood slowly, coming to my full height before her. She looked me over, starting at my feet. As her attention traveled up my body, it was as if her gaze burned my flesh. When she looked at my hard cock and licked her lips, I could not control my reaction, a loud rumble coming from my chest.

The sound caused her to look up at once, her head tilted back. Her long hair flowed down her back nearly to her waist, and I stepped forward, close enough to raise my hand and reach behind her. I tangled my fingers in her hair and held her in place as I leaned down, towering over her.

"You must go. Now."

"What if I don't?" Her eyes flashed with challenge, and I tugged at the drank strands, watched as her eyes dilated and her breathing sped at the dominant touch.

"I will not be gentle. I will bend you over the bed and fuck you until you beg me to stop. And then I will fuck you until you beg me to make you come again." Holding her head in place, I leaned in close and pressed my face to the curve of her neck, breathed her scent deep into my lungs, the tip of my cock pressed to her stomach, precum sliding over her skin, marking her. "You will take Varin into your mouth and pleasure him as I fill you with my cock. You will serve both of us until I give you permission to stop."

She gasped but didn't move to pull away. She stood still, yet I sensed no fear, only...need. Anticipation. Lust.

Truly she was magnificent. Perfect. Sexy.

Mine.

Shaking with the need to bend her to my will, mark her, fuck her, claim her, I held perfectly still. One movement and I would lose control, take her body as I had threatened.

The silence stretched as Varin moved closer to us. I knew he would prevent me from hurting our mate, his mind locked to mine for so long I could practically read his thoughts as easily as he could read mine. Share pain, and pleasure. He moved to stand behind her, trapping her body between our two, much larger frames. He intentionally tested her resolve, pushed her limits, called her bluff. She was small. Weak. Female. This would frighten—

"Okay." The nearly breathless sound of her voice took a moment to register.

"What?"

With a coy look at me through her lashes, she twisted her head to the side in a silent demand that I release her. I did so, shocked by the desire flooding my mind. Not mine nor Varin's, but *hers*.

On silent feet, she slipped to the side and out from between us. Varin and I stared as she walked to the bed and stood facing it before laying her belly and breasts down on the soft surface, ass facing me, legs spread wide, feet barely reaching the floor. She was on the tips of her toes, and I knew when I pushed into her wet heat from behind, her feet would no longer touch the floor. Her soaked pussy glistened as she tilted her head to look over at the two of us. "I'm not tall enough to reach you if you stand up, Varin, so you'll have to lie down on the bed."

By the gods, was she *offering herself* to me? To my cock, just as I'd imagined? Did she truly intend to take Varin into her mouth and suck his cock as I had instructed?

Was she obeying my command? Submitting to my desire?

No female had ever done so, not before my service in the Coalition Fleet, not during my youth on Prillon Prime, and definitely not since I'd become contaminated, further dishonored. Sex had always been about bargaining and power plays. Appeasing the curiosity of the few females brave enough to fuck a member of the

Arcas family, brutality, betrayal, madness, and murder our family legacy.

She laid her breasts flat and lifted a hand to her hip, caressed the curve of her ass and pulled her rounded cheek to the side, further exposing her core.

My balls drew up tight, painfully swollen as my body processed her intention faster than my mind.

"I'm going to fuck that ass when we claim you." Varin moved quickly to the opposite side of the bed, climbing up to recline on his side, positioned perfectly so that the tip of his hard cock was directly in front of her mouth.

She did not respond to his statement. Instead she leaned down and sucked the tip of his bulbous cock into her mouth.

A rush of sensual heat flooded my mind, pushing the remnants of my confusion aside. The Hive implants still buzzed in my head. My muscles ached and burned under the constant attack from the microscopic muscle augmentations. My very bones felt as if they were breaking in half. None of it mattered. My focus narrowed to her. Her mouth. The feeling Varin experienced as she worked him with one hand and sucked him deep, his tip hitting the back of her throat. He arched his back to move closer and she moaned.

"You aren't going to get another invitation, brother. She can't speak at the moment." Varin actually laughed, the sound foreign yet tugging at long dead memories of better days.

Let her go. Walk away. Do not make her suffer your dishonor. Your failure.

And yet her pussy glistened in invitation. The musky

scent of her desire had me fighting for air. For control. If I were an honorable warrior, I would deny myself. Protect her.

"Fuck her, Thomar. Slide your cock into her pussy and fill her with your seed. Fuck her. Make her come. Give her pleasure. You can feel guilty about it later."

Varin was an ass. Yet he spoke the truth. I could feel her agreement, her resolve in our mental bond through the collars.

I moved with augmented speed, faster than even Varin could, and positioned the tip of my cock at her wet entrance. Stopped.

This was wrong. I was going to die and leave her unprotected.

No. Varin would claim her. Keep her. He had to. I looked at him, at the dazed expression on his face, his half-closed eyes. "You must vow to me that you will claim her. Protect her. I will make her ours, I will accept the match, but you must vow to me you will be her true mate once I am gone."

Varin's eyes opened and he stared at me as he affirmed his vow. "I am your second. I am hers."

Yes. Of course. That was our way, our law. Warriors always mated as a pair. Too many of us died in the war. With two mates, a female and any children were never left alone to fend for themselves. Never abandoned. Once I was gone, Varin would choose his own second and this female, my female, would be cared for. Pleasured. Protected. As was right.

Our mate wiggled her ass and tried to push back and force me inside her small body. I did not need to be careful, for she had already enjoyed Varin's attentions and his cock was nearly as large as mine.

Placing one hand on each side of her bottom, I lifted her slightly to get a better angle.

Shifted my stance. Tilted my hips.

"You did nothing to prepare her for you." I rubbed the rounded globes of her ass and looked my fill of her tight backside where I knew the ATB device had been implanted during the bride center processing and transport. Always ready with anything we needed.

And now I wanted her to know who was fucking her, filling both holes because I chose to, because she had given herself to me and I wanted to play. To make her come. Make her squirm and beg and lose control.

I bent low and covered her back as I activated the device in her sweet ass, set the anal trainer to its smallest setting.

She moaned, a flood of shock and craving hitting both Varin and I through the collars.

She lifted her lips from Varin's cock long enough to speak. "Oh God. What is that?"

I ran my palm along her side, caressed her breast, her waist, the curve of her hip and thigh. "That is your anal training device. Has anyone taken you in the ass before? As Varin will when we claim you?"

"No." She was panting. I reached between us with my roving hand and tested her pussy with my fingers. She was soaked. Wet. More than ready.

"Do you like my toy in your ass? Filling you up?"

"Yes." She did not lie, and I rewarded her by rubbing her clit. She wiggled beneath me, desperate for more.

"If you want me to fuck you, suck Varin deep. Make sure he hits the back of your throat."

Varin groaned as she followed my orders, both of us experiencing the tightness of her tongue and mouth, the suction tempting Varin to lose himself and give her his seed.

"Do not come, Varin. Not until I command it." I shifted position and pulled her pussy lips open wide so I could place the tip of my cock at her entrance. With a slow, steady motion, I slid deep inside her pussy. Bottomed out as she shuddered and moaned.

Her heat wrapped around me until the sensation coming from my cock drowned the rest of me. The training device had filled her ass and made her pussy that much tighter. More rigid.

"Fuck." I had to move. Fuck her. Rub my hard cock around inside her. Fill her so full she'd never want another.

Irrational. Possessive. I didn't resist, stopped trying to fight it.

In. Out. I let go of her bottom with one hand to grab hold of her hair. I tugged at the soft strands, moved her head a bit faster over Varin's cock, synced her movement sucking him deep with mine as I filled her wet pussy from behind. All three of our minds synced as one through the collars. I didn't recognize the deep rumble coming from my throat.

"Fuck. I'm going to come." Varin spoke through clenched teeth.

"Not yet." I felt his pleasure building, the hard edge of his desire about to explode and pull me over the edge with him. Pulling on her hair, I carefully lifted her off his cock and gently lowered her head to the table so that her cheek rested flat and I could see her eyes, her parted lips, the flushed face of our beautiful female panting as I fucked her harder. Faster. Her body rocking back and forth on top of the bed as I pumped in and out of her.

"Yes. Don't stop." Her voice was hoarse with need.

I shifted my hips and changed my angle, stuffed her full. She moaned.

"That hurts. So good. God, it's so good."

I stopped moving, buried balls-deep and held her in place. Submissive. Trapped.

Mine.

"You are in pain?"

"No. Yes. No. Just don't stop."

I stroked her back with a soothing hand, neck to ass as I held perfectly still. "I said you would beg."

"I'm not."

My smile stretched across my face slowly; it had been so long, so damn long since I'd worn such an expression. "Not yet. You aren't begging yet." I placed a finger near her ass, touched the ATB device, and made it grow to the next, slightly larger size inside her body.

She moaned, her fingers digging into the medical bed, trying to hold on to something. Anything.

Her efforts were futile. The bedding was hard and her hands were weak. Small. Delicate.

I wanted to feel them wrapped around my cock. Stroking my hair. I wanted to know that something so fragile and feminine did not fear to touch me.

Angry at myself for the weakness, I pulled back.

Thrust into her. Deep. Hard. Again. When her body rocked too far forward, I placed my free hand on her back and held her in place for my thrusts, the larger ATB pressing down on my hard cock inside her pussy like a relentless fist.

"Oh God."

"I am your god now."

A thrill went through her at my words, and I filed the information away for later. This sassy female liked my hand holding her in place, liked to feel me pulling her hair. Her pussy spasmed with each tug on her head. She wanted me to dominate her body, pleasure her, take control so she did not need to think, only feel.

I pulled a bit harder on her hair, pleased when she moaned in pleasure and a flood of wetness surrounded my cock. "Take Varin deep. When he comes, you will come."

Gasping for air, she did not resist when I held her down at the waist with one hand and used the other to lift her head into position above Varin's cock once more. "Varin, show her what you like."

His hand replaced mine as he guided her over him. Faster. Deeper.

He would not last long.

I slapped our mate's ass, testing her. She gasped. Cried out, the sound muffled around Varin's cock as I smacked her soft ass once more.

"Do not come until you have Varin's seed on your tongue."

My command made her body jerk, her pussy clamp down on my cock as she sucked on Varin with more pressure, swirled his tip with her tongue. Squeezed his balls with her small hand.

I knew all this even as he experienced what I felt as I fucked her, my cock sliding in and out of her, faster and faster. Normal Prillon collars gave mates a sense of emotions. Thanks to the Hive's experiments, Varin and I were not normal. I felt what he felt. What I felt. My mind was overloaded with the pleasure of both her mouth and her pussy, the sight of her taking Varin in her mouth and Varin's vision of me filling her from behind.

We spiraled quickly, Varin and I losing control. There was nothing but *her.*

"Come now." I smacked her bottom one more time as Varin's orgasm rushed through him like a supernova exploding into dark, empty space.

Our mate swallowed him down, her scream of pleasure muffled as her body went rigid. She began to shake. The pulsing spasms of her pussy walls, her orgasm, forced me to lose control. I came. Hard. So fucking hard it hurt.

I gave her my seed, my body, my protection.

When I could move, I stroked her curves as gently as I could. I set the ATB device back to its normal setting, ready to provide more training to stretch her ass or lube for Varin's cock on demand. Best fucking invention ever.

I moved my hand in soothing strokes up and down her back to calm her, let her know she was safe. Protected. Precious. That she was mine. Ours.

For now.

Danika, Personal Quarters, Two Days Later

ot, solid muscle pressed to my back, Thomar lay wrapped around me, his arm over my waist, holding me close.

Blinking away my exhaustion, I opened my eyes to find Varin lying before me, his shoulder my pillow, my hand resting on his chest as if it belonged there.

Naked, surrounded and protected by my mates, my muscles felt like heated candle wax, still warm and pliable but with no strength. After Thomar had wrapped me up like a burrito in the black sheet and carried me out of the medical station, Varin clearing our path to what I later learned was our new private quarters, they'd fed me. Bathed me. Fucked me again. Ordered me to sleep. Awakened me with a mouth on my pussy and another at my breast. We hadn't left the room in nearly two days, and we'd barely spoken more than a handful of sentences to one another.

Seemed that once my guys decided to get naked, they couldn't stop. Not that I was complaining. Except for the fact that I wasn't going to be able to walk right for a week. The thing in my ass, this *Anal Training Box,* as they called it, had filled me up over and over, getting bigger, stretching me open. And holy shit, it wasn't nearly as big as Varin's cock would feel. Not yet.

I was sore and bruised and used up in the most delicious way. I hurt. My core had been empty for a long time. When I broke her in, I did it with style. I didn't care if I was sore or tired or hungry. I'd never been more relieved in my life.

My mate, Thomar, had decided to keep me. Claim me. I felt the shift in his mind the moment he'd made the decision, his cock buried deep as he held me bent over the bed in that medical room. I'd nearly cried with relief. I didn't have to try to find a new mate in thirty days. And despite what the two wardens had told me when I was still on Earth, I didn't trust the "system." The law, the bureaucracy had failed me over and over in my lifetime. That was just on Earth. What could possibly be more confusing and convoluted than the laws governing a Coalition of Planets with over two hundred *worlds*?

Thomar still intended to die. I could feel the intention every time he touched me, but I would have some time to come up with a solution. Now that I'd had a taste of them both, there was no way I was giving up on him. I understood pain. Suffering. Torture. Knew that Varin suffered torture as well as watching someone he cared about suffer. In my opinion that was ten times worse than experiencing it oneself.

Somehow he was protecting me from the worst of his mental struggles. I could feel my guys' emotions, but many times the last two days I had suspected that Thomar and Varin could actually read each other's thoughts, like full telepathy, vampire-movie style. Many times I'd seen first Thomar, then Varin wince as if in pain or stop moving simultaneously, becoming frozen statues as they dealt with something going on inside their heads.

I didn't know what to do. Touching them seemed to help bring them back to reality, but sometimes that didn't work and I had to simply wait.

Waiting terrified me.

Something was wrong with them, and it was serious. They refused to say anything more than what they'd already told me, that Thomar and Varin were linked by mating collars that the Hive had imbedded in their spines. That there was no way to remove the collars without killing them. That the only way for Thomar to spare both me and Varin a lifetime of suffering was for Thomar to die and set Varin free.

But not until *after* Thomar formally claimed me with Varin in a mating ceremony.

Which left me with the option to refuse them until I had this figured out. Thirty days suddenly did not seem like long enough. I needed more time.

Time to call in the big guns. I was going to go see that golden doctor myself and find out exactly what I was dealing with.

Alone. No bullshit. No overly protective, scowling

mates glaring down the doctor. If there was a way to save Thomar, I was going to find it. I very much liked these two. I wasn't in love with them, not yet anyway. Not that I would know. I'd never been in love before. The only person I'd ever really loved was my little brother. I'd fought for him, too, and been sent to prison as a result.

I'd do it again in a heartbeat.

"I can feel your upset, female. Tell me what hurts you so I may take care of it." Thomar's rough voice came from behind me, and I smiled as his hand moved over my thigh, traced the contour of my hip and waist, moved up and down in a soothing glide of male heat.

"Just thinking about the past. It's nothing. I left it behind on Earth."

"Apparently you did not." Varin was awake now as well, his free hand crossed over his chest so he could stroke my cheek.

Holy shit, being surrounded, adored, and soothed by two massive warriors was heaven on Earth. No, on The Colony. Heaven on The Colony.

How weird.

"Does this planet have an actual name? Or is it literally called The Colony and that's it?"

Varin's thumb traced my bottom lip. "This planet has a designation number in the Interstellar Coalition of Planets database. However, as far as I know, before we colonized the surface and began our mining operations, the planet had no other name."

Somehow that seemed sad to me. No idea why. Just sad.

Thomar squeezed my hip. "You will not succeed in

distracting me. I will know what troubles you. You will tell me now. We saw your file, we know you have killed a human, as Lady Rone stated, 'in cold blood.' You will tell us why you were forced to such an act. Who hurt you? Tell us everything."

Bossy much? "Why do you assume someone hurt me?"

Varin cleared his throat. "We can feel you, Danika. You are not violent or aggressive. You are a female. Weak and in need of protection. We demand to know what happened to you so we can comfort and protect you."

"Speak," Thomar ordered.

"No. I don't want to talk about it." No freaking way. That was a deep, dark rabbit hole I had no intention of visiting again. Ever. I had blood on my hands, but my brother was safe and happy and had just started college. He was going to be all right, and I was finally free. So yeah, over and done. Not going back there. "I left Earth for a reason. The past is the past."

"You are my mate. I am your primary male. You must obey my orders, or I will be unable to protect you."

"You can't protect me from my own memories."

"And yet that is what you intend to do for me? Do you believe yourself to be more powerful than I?"

Oh shit. That was a loaded question if ever I heard one. "No."

"Then I order you to tell me. Now."

"No."

Thomar's cock grew hard behind me as if my defiance was turning him on. Shit.

"Varin, kiss our mate. Do not stop until she is screaming."

Varin's hand froze on my cheek, and he shifted under me, moving down so that our faces were aligned on the bed. His cock, too, had become hard. Full. Leaked a drop of pre-cum.

"Thomar, I—"

His cock slid into my wet heat from behind and I gasped. He moved my leg up and back so that my ankle was behind his thigh, my pussy open. Stuffed full of his hard length. Exposed.

He moved. His cock rubbing me in all the right— tender—places. In. Out.

He thrust deep. Hard. Fast.

"Thomar!"

"Varin, I gave you an order."

With a wicked grin, Varin locked his mouth to mine, stealing my breath and my protest. His hand moved from my cheek to my clit, and he began to stroke me as Thomar stroked in and out of me from behind. Thomar's hand traveled away from my hip to tease and roll my nipples, tugging until they were hard peaks. I moaned, my back arching as Varin varied his fingers' speed on my clit. Faster. Slower.

Thomar placed his hand on my neck, gently held me in place for Varin's rough kiss. The combination of tenderness and rough touches from my mates drove me out of my mind. All thoughts of my past, gone. There was only Thomar and Varin. This moment. Their lips and hands and cocks.

Varin shifted again, moved so that the tip of his cock

rubbed my clit. I reached down to touch him but found his hand already in the way, a firm fist over his hard length as he rubbed the thick end along my clit over and over. He was stroking off using my body, my wetness coating his tip, making him slide more easily.

His kiss drove me mad as he moved his tongue in time to his rubbing. Thomar adjusted his thrusts to match, squeezed my neck. The thrill that moved through me at being held still, motionless, completely under his control, was absurd. I loved knowing he was in command. Loved that I could not move, only take what they would give me. I should be protesting, not melting into them, ready to beg for more.

My body was exhausted, my pussy swollen, overly sensitized to every touch.

My orgasm built, one small spasm followed by two, my core so inflamed I could feel the individual muscles that lined my pussy as they jerked and tried to lock Thomar's cock inside me.

I held off my release, barely, willing to wait for the bigger payoff.

"You hold yourself back."

Varin's kiss did not relent. I could not answer Thomar. Didn't need to. He knew.

With a deep groan that made me think of a tiger's growl, he placed a hand on my inner thigh and pulled my knee up higher, farther back. Spread me open wider.

Increased his speed. Harder. Deeper. Faster.

Varin matched him.

I screamed, the sound of my release caught in Varin's

mouth, his lips dominating mine, taking all of me and demanding more.

Giving them everything I could, I moaned as the orgasm went on and on, Varin's release coating my leg as Thomar filled my pussy with his seed. Their combined pleasure through the collars created a loop of erotic chaos in my mind for long minutes as my pussy spasmed and wept for them. For more.

When it was over, we lay panting and spent as I fought back tears. I was in pain, my heart aching, eyes burning, but I did not know why. Was I too vulnerable? Too weak? Angry? Lost?

Lost. I felt lost. I was falling for my mates, Varin and Thomar. And I didn't want to, not if one of them was determined to leave me behind.

Nothing good ever came from loving someone else. I'd learned that the hard way.

Thomar's cock slipped free, and I felt the press of his lips to the back of my head. My shoulder. "Now, mate, you will tell us what troubles you so we can take care of it."

I sighed. Not this again. Stubborn Prillon males. "Right after you describe for me, in detail, everything the Hive did to you while you were their prisoner. Every pain you suffered."

"Never. We would never burden you with our suffering. That is not our way."

"Well, it's not my way either."

"You must share yourself with us," Varin insisted, his thumb stroking a wayward tear from my cheek. "Tell us, Danika. Now. We need to know everything."

"No, you don't. And right now I'm going to take a shower."

Varin's wicked grin was back, but I shook my head.

"Alone. Okay? I need some space." I slid down to the foot of the huge bed, leaving them staring at me as if confused.

Varin's hurt look followed me into the bathing room, but I didn't know what else to do. I needed answers, a plan, and I wasn't going to get either of those losing my mind and all control in bed with those two, no matter how tempting the idea may be.

I locked the door and pressed a control panel the way I'd seen Varin or Thomar do when they wanted food or other items delivered to our rooms, and when the golden doctor, Surnen, had called to check up on all of us. He'd insisted on speaking to me, under the guise of medical safety. Thomar had been incensed, but I placed a hand on his chest and told the doctor I was fine, that my mates were taking excellent care of me. That had calmed him down. He did *not* like anyone accusing him of not caring for me properly. He had a massive chip on his shoulder about his honor and providing for a mate. Another confusing thing I needed to find out about.

He'd been so happy with my assurances to the doctor, he'd fucked my brains out. Again. Varin had been only too eager to assist.

"Lady Arcas, control room. How may we assist?" The voice coming through the speaker in the bathroom seemed especially loud but successfully jolted me from my jaunt down sexy memory lane. I did need something.

"Can you find the other Earth girls and tell them I'd like to meet them, please?"

"One moment." I waited, hopping from foot to foot as the scent of my mates and hot, sweaty sex hung around me like a cloud. The smell made me think about Thomar's cock, Varin's hands, the taste of them, the way they touched me.

Shit. I crossed my legs as my pussy throbbed. Again.

I was as bad as my guys were. Maybe worse. Totally insatiable.

"Lady Arcas, I have contacted Lady Rone. She said to inform you that she will come to your quarters in half an hour."

I slumped in relief. I only had to resist my mates for thirty minutes. If I stayed locked in here, I could do it. If I left this room and they touched me? I was a goner. Totally not fair.

"Okay. Thank you. Tell her I'll be ready."

"Very well. Let us know if you need anything else. Control room out."

I hurried through my shower, making sure to wash everywhere. Everywhere, everywhere. My mates were very thorough lovers and had not left the smallest part of me unexplored.

When thirty minutes had passed, I had dressed in a pair of soft, green cotton pants and an oversize cream-colored sweatshirt. The S-Gen machine the guys had shown me was fabulous, and I had created fluffy socks, my favorite athletic shoes, and a bra that actually fit, which was a miracle all on its own. Everything that touched my skin was soft and warm, not the rough, industrial fabric they made us wear in prison. I pulled my still damp hair up into a twist and clipped it in place with my newly S-Gen-created hair clip. I glanced at myself in the mirror and put my hands on my hips. Twisted this way and that to get a good look.

I looked good. Normal. Happy.

"I could get used to this." I spoke to the woman in the mirror, the one with flushed cheeks and swollen lips and a glow about her I'd never seen before.

A pleasant ringing tone sounded in the other room, and I hurried to open the bathroom door.

Too late. Thomar stood, bare-ass naked in front of the open door, hands on his hips and scowl on his face.

"What the fuck do you want?" I peeked around his hips to see two armed guards standing before him, unfazed by his lack of attire.

"We are here to ensure Lady Rone's safety."

"Lady Rone is not here. Go. Leave us."

My heart sank a bit as I worried Thomar would scare them off. "I called her. They're here for me." I approached Thomar slowly and placed my hand on the back of his shoulder. "It's okay. I wanted to meet the other Earth girls."

Thomar's entire body was tense, and I felt the anger, the chaos in his mind.

Varin moved from where he'd been reclined in bed to stand on his other side. "Thomar, stand down. They are friends."

"They will take our mate." A shiver raced over his body, and I winced in pain as a flash of agony, of rage stabbed into my mind through the collars. I had not felt this when we were alone, when Thomar was relaxed.

The two Prillon warriors took a step back and brought their weapons forward, not that the weapons would stop Thomar. They looked like baby-sized ray guns from a bad sci-fi movie.

Their motion sent Thomar another step closer to the edge, his reaction like boiling water inside my head. I gasped in pain, my fingers clawing into his back as I wobbled on my feet. God. How did he live with this?

Moving slowly, I clung to him as I shifted under his arm, along his side, to stand in front of him, between the other Prillons and my very angry, very volatile mate. "Thomar, it's okay. I promise. I'm okay." I wrapped one arm around his waist and squeezed as close as I could, pressing my body against him. With my free hand, I reached up to grab his chin. Gently, I tugged. "Look at me."

He lowered his gaze, the chaos still churning in his mind. When our gazes locked, I saw the despair there, the shame. He could not control himself. Found his lack unforgivable. I knew this because his emotions came through the collar as clear as bells ringing in the wind.

"Thomar, give yourself time. I am going to meet the other women from Earth. Hopefully I can make some friends. I am perfectly safe with her guards. Okay? I'll be back."

"Two hours. Then I come for you."

It was a start, and I didn't want to push him. I knew he was fighting himself to let me out of his sight at all. The doctor and Varin had not exaggerated the level of his

Hive implants or his mental and emotional struggles. "Okay. Two hours."

"I shall set my comm. She won't be late." Lady Rone stepped forward from somewhere behind the guards. She'd been standing back, probably waiting to see what would happen with Thomar and his...condition. "I give you my word of honor that she will be safe. My mates do not allow females on The Colony to be in danger."

"As proper warriors should not. If anything happens, I will come for them."

"Thomar!" Had he seriously just threatened to kill the leaders of this place?

Lady Rone grinned at him, her complete lack of concern the only thing preventing me from having a stroke on the spot. "I'll let them know."

"Do so. Two hours."

I stepped back to go with the guards, but Thomar grabbed me and kissed me. Hard. Deep. Like he couldn't live without me, like the gods themselves demanded he claim me. He was totally dominant, aggressive, possessive. Everything inside me went nuclear, and I had wrapped my arms around him before I realized I had lost track of where I was standing.

I heard a woman clear her throat.

Oh shit.

Fighting for air, I broke contact and stared up into Thomar's fierce gaze. "I'll be back in two hours. I'll be fine. I want to go meet the other women from Earth. It will make me happy."

He shuddered, but I knew through the collars that he had control of himself now. "Go. Do not be late."

"You're really bossy, you know that?"

His smile was feral. Wild. I stepped back and smiled at Lady Rone. She held out her hand, and I shook it.

"Forget that." She pulled me into a hug, and I hugged her back. Hard. "Welcome to The Colony, Danika. We've been dying to meet you." She glanced over her shoulder, back at Thomar, as she led me away with an arm around my shoulder. "Had to wait because your mates kept you locked in your room." Her words were overly loud and intended for ears other than my own.

I glanced back to gauge Thomar's reaction. I shouldn't have looked.

Arms crossed, his massive body covered in geometric designs, his cock full and free and pointing at me as if he wanted to follow me down the hallway. There wasn't an ounce of embarrassment in his body. I knew because I could feel him. And Varin, who was behind him, flooded with relief. Hope. Exhaustion. He was tired. So tired of struggling, of feeling Thomar's pain. Of absorbing so much pain as his own so Thomar could survive another day. Another hour.

I had to help them both. Varin with his loyal, loving heart. He was solid as a rock, strong, Thomar's anchor and now, my new family's foundation. And Thomar, who fought for control over his aggressive nature, his warrior's instincts, turned up to the maximum and beyond by Hive integrations and two years of torture.

How had they survived?

Thomar was still watching me, so I grinned and shouted back down the corridor, "Stop showing off,

Thomar. Get some clothes on. I don't want the other women going after my man."

I felt a thrill pass through him at my words. "Who is bossy now, mate?"

"I am. Get dressed. Stop showing off your gorgeous body."

He stepped back with a grin on his face, and I heard him brag to Varin as the door to our quarters slid closed, "Our mate finds me gorgeous."

The two guards finally relaxed, lowering their weapons. They turned to face me and introduced themselves.

"Lady Arcas, I am Marz." The male was golden, much like the doctor. He inclined his head.

"And I am Tyran."

Lady Rone crossed her arms and looked them over, but spoke to Tyran, "I see Maxim sent the big guns."

"Of course," Tyran smiled and his rich, dark skin and dark eyes could bring any girl to her knees.

My confusion must have shown on my face because Lady Rone took my arm and turned me toward the corridor, away from Thomar and Varin. "Tyran has so many integrations he can tear an Atlan beast into pieces with his bare hands. He's the strongest male on The Colony."

Walking now, I glanced back over my shoulder at what I thought was a very normal-looking Prillon warrior. "Really?"

"Yes," Tyran confirmed. "You will meet my mate in a few minutes. She will be happy to brag about her magnificent male. I am undefeated in the fighting pits. I look forward to shoving Thomar's face into the dust."

I burst into laughter and looked at Lady Rone. "Are they all like that, Lady Rone?"

She smiled. "Call me Rachel. And yes. Every single one of them."

I looked back at Marz. "What about you?"

"I am not as strong as Tyran. He has more integrations. I am not mated and my second is dead."

"I'm sorry." Damn. Better be careful what I ask around here. Seems these guys only knew how to be blunt and to the point. I had no idea what to say to his revelations. Great way to put my foot in my mouth.

"My bride will come."

Rachel looked back at him. "Yes, she will. Hold on, Marz. You'll get an Earth girl. I have good instincts for this kind of thing."

He inclined his head but said nothing. Rachel wrapped her hand around my elbow and rubbed my soft sweater. "You got the S-Gen thing down. I need some lessons."

"No problem."

She laughed. "I knew I was going to like you. Let's go. The others are waiting."

7

Varin, Medical Station, The Colony

Thomar sat next to me on the medical bed as Dr. Surnen ran his scanners over each of us in turn.

"Well?" I asked.

Dr. Surnen's face gave nothing away. The warrior was pure fucking stone. "There have been subtle frequency disruptions."

"What does that mean?" Thomar asked.

"I do not know. I will need to run more tests."

"Fuck your tests. We all know what is happening here. How long do I have?" Thomar slid off the exam bed to stand and clenched his fists, his tone causing more than one of the doctor's assistants to scurry to the opposite side of the large room.

Confused by the question, I looked at the doctor, who

held Thomar's gaze without flinching. "At the current rate of decays, seven to ten days before you…"

"What?" I stood as well, feeling as if my heart had just exploded inside my chest. "What do you mean, seven days? What the fuck are you talking about?"

Thomar's guilt and regret hit me through the collars until I nearly fell to my knees with it. "Place me on the IC's strike list. Give me seven days."

No. Just fucking no. The Intelligence Core's strike list was for warriors willing to accept missions where there was little to no hope of coming back alive. Warriors or beasts or fighters from the other worlds who already knew they were going to die. Suicide missions.

"What are you not telling me?" I asked Thomar.

Thomar looked at the doctor and gave a small nod of his head, then leaned back to rest his hips against the exam table and crossed his arms over his chest. The doctor looked from him to me and cleared his throat.

"Thomar's body is reacting to the modified collar and the surrounding Hive implants."

"Reacting? How, exactly?"

"His body is rejecting the integrations and the surrounding tissues are dying, causing decay and sepsis, infection that has spread into his bloodstream." He looked at Thomar. "I will need you to spend no less than one hour each day in the ReGen pod if you want to be functional for the IC mission."

"There has to be something you can do." I was not losing Thomar now, not after everything we had survived. Now that we had Danika. We'd been closer than brothers since we were old enough to walk. I would not allow him to give up now.

"I am still running tests."

A growl filled the room, and I realized it had come from me. I clenched my hands at my sides. "What did I just say about tests?"

Thomar interrupted before the doctor could speak. "I can feel myself dying, Varin. The doctor has tried everything he knows to do. Nothing helps."

The golden Prillon doctor cleared his throat. "I am sorry. I will continue looking for an answer. Thomar's genetics are slightly different than the standard Prillon."

"He's fucking royal."

"I am not."

"Your family is one of the original royal lines. I don't give a fuck what some asshole ancestor of yours did. You are the most honorable warrior I know."

Thomar remained silent but our bond was strong. I felt his friendship and loyalty through the collars. His despair came at me as well, like a black cloud threatening to drown me, which made me eager to punch the doctor.

Unproductive but satisfying.

"I am running some experiments with Lady Rone." He raised a hand to hold us both back from whatever reaction we were about to have. "As I told you, Thomar, the frequency of your collar implant changed once I removed your other integrations. I believe your body must have been having a reaction to the collars while you were still a captive and the Hive fitted you with additional devices to counteract the problem."

"What does that mean?" I asked.

The doctor looked at me. "When you both arrived, I removed all the integrations I could without endangering your health, as I always do. I believe that with those gone, there is nothing mitigating Thomar's natural response. His body is rejecting the modified collar and spinal integrations, destroying the circuits and eating away at the collar itself. Perhaps the reaction is releasing toxins. If my theory is correct, that would explain your constant pain. The integrations in your brain tissue are most likely degrading as well."

"Have you seen something like this before?"

"Only in the Atlans. It is the reason most Atlans do not survive the integration process. Their bodies' natural defense attacks many of the Hive integrations."

I rolled my eyes and looked at my friend. "I knew you were part beast, you bastard."

Thomar actually grinned, which was a huge improvement over his previous glower. "No. I can trace my Prillon bloodlines back thousands of years."

"Oh yes, your royalness. To a fucking beast."

The doctor chuckled and we both returned our attention to him. "So, what do we do?" I asked.

Dr. Surnen shook his head. "I'm not sure yet. As I said, Lady Rone and I are working on it."

"Lady Rone?" Thomar asked.

Dr. Surnen nodded. "She is a scientist and researcher. Quite talented. She has saved many lives since her arrival here. She looks at things from a refreshingly odd angle." He pointed to a strange piece of equipment resting on a counter in the far corner of the room. "That is her workstation. She uses the same equipment she worked with on Earth. It is ancient technology. Inefficient, but she insists it helps her think."

We all stared in silence at the black contraption with nobs and peeping holes for the eyes. Earth females were unique, no doubt. Now that I had one of my own, I would do whatever I needed to in order to keep her. Protect her.

Claim her.

"So, we have seven days?" I spoke freely, knowing Thomar would prefer the truth, as I did.

Dr. Surnen shook his head. "I believe so, with daily time in a ReGen pod. Much beyond that and I fear he will lose his mind."

————

Danika

"Here. I'm guessing you need this." Lady Rone—Rachel, as she insisted I call her—placed a tray loaded with piping hot food, coffee, tea, water, and a strange device that looked like a sci-fi remote control of some kind in the center of the table. I had no idea what it operated.

The scent of the food hit me, and my stomach rumbled. With a laugh, I dug into the meal as she leaned back in a chair sipping on her own cup of hot tea. Neither of us spoke as I shoveled food into my mouth like a starving lunatic, but I realized I really was hungry. And thirsty. And exhausted.

And happy about all three. When I finished, I sat back and smiled. "Thanks. I needed that."

Her grin was infectious. "I am mated to a pair of Prillons. Believe me, I understand."

When I was done blushing, my curiosity came roaring to life.

"How long have you been here?" I asked.

"Three years, give or take."

"Wow." Three years. That was... "That's a long time."

"Seems like yesterday."

"Are you happy here?"

"Very." She leaned forward and lifted the remote control thing from the tray. "This is called a ReGen wand. It's one of the technologies the Coalition has not shared with Earth." She pushed some buttons, and the top half of the wand turned a bright green. She held it out to me. "Place this on your lap, right against your body."

I did as she asked. Instantly my lower half became warm and tingly, the soreness leaving my core and my thighs. "What?" I looked down, shocked.

"Keep it in your room. I have one. We all do. They are big, our mates, and sometimes a little extra healing goes a long way."

When the tingling stopped, I lifted the wand to the side of my head where I had the beginnings of a stress headache. The same sensation filled my skull—my face and sinuses, everything felt...good. "Wow. What else can this thing do?" I moved it to my knee, which ached pretty much every day since I'd taken a fall in gym class when I was fourteen.

"It will heal most small wounds, colds. Anything that makes you feel like hell or causes lingering pain. If something major happens, they have full-sized ReGen pods in medical that will heal major trauma. If you can make it to a ReGen pod alive, they can pretty much heal anything. It's like laying in a coffin, but it works."

"Holy shit." I put my hand over my mouth. "Sorry. I curse like a sailor."

"Or a federal prisoner."

I froze, wondering where this was going.

She held up her hands. "Don't worry. I served time, too. You'll get no judgment from me."

"You did?" I looked her over. Kind, compassionate look in her eyes. No scars that I could see. She was soft. "White-collar crime? What did you do?"

"I was framed, caught up in a pharmaceutical scandal where a lot of people died."

"Only one person died because of me." I moved the ReGen wand to my shoulder and melted back into my chair in her office. God, this thing really did work miracles. This shoulder had bothered me since I'd had it nearly twisted off by a big bitch on the inside my second night in prison.

"I bet he deserved it."

The words startled me, but she wasn't wrong. "How did you know it was a man?"

"Lucky guess?" She looked at me over the top of her teacup. "And as the governor's mate and part of the medical team, I am one of the few people with full access to your file."

"He did. Doesn't make it right."

"Doesn't make it wrong, either. I wanted to meet you first, before the others."

"Decide if I was a threat?"

She looked guilty but not contrite. I would not get an apology from her. "I protect what's mine, just like you did. Like our mates do."

"And? What have you decided about me?" I should not care. Should. *Not.* But I did. A lot.

"I think we'll be great friends. And I believe you will be happy here. Thomar and Varin are honorable warriors."

"They are." I wanted to ask her about Thomar's condition. She'd said she was part of the medical team. She had to know exactly what was going on with him. How to fix him. I didn't get the chance to ask because the door to her office slid open and four women burst into the room, laughing and stumbling over each other like children.

"Oh my God! It's true! I can't believe you're here!" The blonde who spoke was dressed like one of the warriors I'd seen monitoring the halls, complete with one of those alien guns on her hip. "I'm Kristen. I'm mated to Tyran and Hunt. Tyran is the hottie who escorted Rachel to your rooms. The super strong one." She put her hands on her hips and smiled at me like we were best friends. "I was informed that I am to tell you that he is a magnificent male and amazing mate."

Laughing now, because I did remember him, very well, I stood and held out my hand. "Danika Gray."

Another blonde shoved Kristen out of the way. "I'm Lindsey. I do PR for The Colony. I'm going to need to interview you as soon as possible. I need photos of you with your mates."

"Okay?"

She grabbed my hand and squeezed. "Oh, we're going to be such good friends. Where are you from?"

"Saratoga Springs, New York." I looked around, expecting more women to be here. "Is this it? Everyone from Earth?"

CJ shoved Kristen out of the way and grabbed me into a hug. "We are the whole show, at least here, on Base 3. Warden Egara is trying to get more brides here, but so far, not much has worked."

"Is that why they made that TV show? *Bachelor Beast*?"

Lindsey pulled CJ off me and grabbed me into her own hug. Tight. After squeezing the air out of my lungs, she let me go and stepped back, her hands still locked around my shoulders. "Did you watch it?"

"Every episode." There wasn't much else to do in prison.

"Did you like it?"

"Loved it. Especially when that first one—"

"Warlord Wulf? He's a sweetheart." She clasped her hands over her heart like she was in love with the Atlan herself.

"Wulf grabbed that makeup artist and locked her in the dressing room with the cameras rolling. That was so sexy."

Kristen was bouncing up and down on the balls of her feet in excitement. "I know! So romantic. And hot. And then Bahre with that poor Quinn and her crazy stalker boyfriend. That one had me on edge. I was so nervous. Governor Maxim thought we might have to go down to Earth and break him out of prison."

"Well, he does have experience." Rachel sounded like

she was teasing, and the others all laughed. There was a story there, I was sure of it.

A gorgeous woman with a friendly smile shifted the baby on her hip, a very big baby. She raised his chubby arm and waved it at me, and the baby smiled the most adorable smile I'd ever seen. Well, except for my baby brother's. "I'm Gabriela. This is Jori. I'm mated to Jorik. He's an Atlan."

"Oh, sorry. I'm mated to Kiel. He's an Elite Hunter from Everis." Lindsey walked to Gabriela and reached for the baby. He held out his arms and went eagerly. She kissed the little one on the cheek and looked back at me. "Come on, you two. We promised Olivia we would bring you to the gardens. She's there with her niece and nephew. And my son, Wyatt and Caroline's twins, CJ and RJ, and Kristen's little girl, Tia. They have probably wrecked the place by now. Oh, and you can meet my mom! She came her with us. You can call her mom or Carla. She'll answer to both."

What? "Your mother has a matched mate here?"

Lindsey burst into laughter. "No. She's not a bride. And she doesn't have one mate, more like a Viken-style group of three very dedicated lovers. She's a maniac. I can barely handle one. They haven't had a formal claiming, but only because she refuses to get married again. Doesn't matter, she's theirs and they are hers."

"Three Vikens?" I had read that Viken males mated in threes.

"Oh no. My mom never does anything by the book. She's with one Viken, one Prillon and an Atlan. They are all older males, about ten years older than Kiel."

"How old is Kiel?"

"I don't know in Earth years. Maybe in his thirties?"

"And your mom?"

"She's just over fifty this year."

"Damn. Good for her." Holy shit. I couldn't even imagine taking on three lovers at that age. But then, I couldn't imagine surviving to forty, let alone fifty. At least not while I was in prison. "How did she hook up with all three of them?"

Lindsey grinned. "Long story. I'll tell you over lunch one of these days. But right now, we have to go save Olivia, my mom and Rachel's mother-in-law from the tiny terrors." She kissed the baby again. "That's what we call you, isn't it? You're all little troublemaking terrors."

The baby squealed and wiggled in Lindsey's arms, clearly pleased at anything said to him that came loaded with love and kisses.

Smart baby.

I looked over my shoulder at Rachel. "Your mother-in-law is here?"

"Yes. Ryston's mother. She relocated to The Colony after his father passed and he refused to leave."

"Because of you?"

She smiled like the cat who ate the canary. "Because of me."

"Does she have a mate here, too?"

"She won't admit anything, but I think she's flirting with one of the males. Taking her time. Making him court her. She was a very important female on Prillon Prime. She's used to being treated like a noblewoman."

"Just one suitor? Not two?"

"Yes. She seems quite taken with one of the Prillons here, but I don't know if he has a second and they haven't made a formal courting agreement. She's not wearing his collar; she's still wearing Ryston's family colors." Rachel shrugged. "She's not talking, so I'm trying to be a good daughter and mind my own business. Ryston will freak and demand to meet the male in the fighting pit. It will be a bunch of drama. These guys are so overprotective. We'll see. She's a fireball, just like Lindsey's mom. I never know what she's going to do."

Fighting pit? That didn't sound good. I had no way to relate. My mom was anything but a fireball. More like a punching bag.

No, that wasn't fair. But my life would have been so different if she'd been stronger. If my dad hadn't died. If she'd never married Martin, the asshole. But then I wouldn't have my little brother, Josh. Had to take the good with the bad.

"Do you all have children?" I was not going to fit in here if I was the only female who had no intention of becoming a mother.

"No. Olivia is raising her niece and nephew. Mikki doesn't have children. Kira either, but she and Angh are at the Academy most of the time. Gwen and Mak are child free, too busy fighting the Hive."

"Yeah, kicking ass and taking names." Kristen sounded proud of her. Like a sister bragging about a sibling.

All the ladies laughed and chatted about the amazing Gwendolyn Fernandez, Hive killer and mate of something called a Forsian, which, according to these women, was even bigger than an Atlan. Which seemed impossible. The ladies moved out of the room, and Rachel rose and indicated I should follow them.

"I didn't realize there were so many children here?" My palms grew clammy, and I felt the color draining from my face. I could do this, right? They were just babies. Little. *Helpless.* Babies.

Shit. I was going to vomit. I moved the green wand thing and held it over my stomach as I stood. I loved kids. Loved them. Loved watching them play and laugh. Loved their innocence. But only in movies. TV commercials. Not in real life.

In real life they suffered. Too much.

I couldn't breathe as memories flooded my system. I hunched over and tried to hide my panic.

Rachel's hand came to rest on my shoulder. "You don't have to go if this is too much. We can be a lot to take in all at once."

"No." I was not going to ruin my chance to make a good first impression with the women I would, hopefully, be spending the rest of my life living with on this planet. "I'm fine."

"All right. Let's go then." She fell in step behind me, and I walked the corridors with my new friends, glad they appeared to be open, kind, and not interested in my past. I didn't want to talk about it. I wanted to forget. All of it.

8

Thomar

*V*arin agreed to stay behind and allow the doctor to run endless tests and scans. I, however, *needed* to see our mate, the instinct both intense and shocking.

Just a few days ago she did not exist to me. And now she was the only reason I cared whether I lived or died. The hours spent in her bed the most peaceful and consuming of my life. She was a gift, an unexpected and final blessing from this fucking shit universe. I'd been born cursed by blood and the sins on my family name. I'd done the one thing I knew how to do well, fight. Destroy. Kill.

The Arcas family had been known for thousands of years as ferocious, merciless warriors. Our bloodline was ancient and feared. Powerful.

Dishonored in the worst way imaginable, abuse of a female, of a treasured mate.

It made no difference that the male in question had been dead more than four hundred years, or that he'd lost his mind. He had betrayed the most sacred trust placed in warriors, protection of those weaker than ourselves. As a result, our family had been distrusted and scorned ever since, our place in the royal families denied all future generations. We could not challenge for the right of Prime, could never rule again.

I had hated the legacy my entire life, yet here I stood, causing my female pain, mental hurt. Anguish. And why? Because I was weak, too weak to walk away once I'd tasted her flesh. Too weak to give her up, to end her suffering, as I should.

I truly was an Arcas after all.

Standing near the edge of The Colony's gardens, I leaned a shoulder against the wall and allowed the sight of my mate to fill me with contentment. She sat on a well-placed stone among the other females, surrounded by smiles and laughter and the squeals of happy children. The setting was one I had never thought to see again.

The surrounding foliage was unfamiliar. I assumed it had been brought from Earth at the females' request. So much green. Too much. Green everywhere. Even the tall trees with their reasonable brown trunks were crowned in green leaves.

The females seemed content, their children running or crawling on a carpet of tiny green spikes that must be much softer than it looked, for even the babies rolled upon it without tears.

As I watched, the two little ones I remembered from the transport room ran to Danika, one at each knee, and proceeded to climb into her lap.

She froze and I felt the first stirrings of unease. Not mine. Hers.

"I CJ," the little female said.

"RJ. I bigger," her twin brother bragged. It was, indeed, true. RJ was quite obviously the son of an Atlan Warlord. A big fucker, too, based on the size of his children.

"Are not."

"Am too."

"No."

"Am too. Duh." RJ stuck out his tongue at his sister, who squeaked in annoyance.

There was that odd word again.

"Mommy! RJ said 'duh.'"

"That's enough, you two." A human female I did not recognize ended the argument as quickly as it had begun, and the twins turned to my mate, their curious gazes locked on her face.

"What's your name?" CJ asked.

"Danika."

"Duh-Nika." RJ muttered, trying it out on his tongue.

"No. No. No," CJ corrected him, then laid her head on Danika's shoulder and reached up blindly, feeling for Danika's hair. Stroked the long strands that I knew, from personal experience, were the softest thing I had ever felt.

Danika's entire body went rigid. Her face showed nothing as emotions exploded within her. Panic. Raw, uncontrollable panic flooded me through the collars.

I rushed toward my mate. Her face had lost all color, and she was fighting to draw air into her body. She gasped, rocked forward and back as if she were in pain.

As gently as I could, I lifted RJ from her lap and placed him on the ground. He raced back toward the female I assumed was his mother. The little girl clung, her fingers wrapped in Danika's hair. Danika appeared to be calm on the outside, but I could feel the alarm in her mind. The anxiety crushing her chest.

"You must get down, little one," I insisted in the softest tone I could manage. CJ burrowed closer, her fist tightening on Danika's hair until removing it would cause my mate pain.

"You're going to have to take a stronger tone with her," her mother instructed.

"I do not wish to frighten the child."

The female burst into laughter. "Their father is an Atlan. They've never lived anywhere but The Colony. Trust me, it takes a lot more than you to scare either one of them."

Danika bolted to her feet, her arm barely holding the child to her. The little girl squealed and released my mate. Moving swiftly, I handed the child to one of the other females, lifted Danika into my arms, and then walked away from the gardens without looking back.

Cradled to my chest, Danika's entire body shook as if she were freezing to death.

"I am here. No one will hurt you."

"Put me down." Panic in the words. Terror. She sounded lost. Alone.

"I have you. You are safe."

"No one is ever safe."

"You are protected now. I give you my word."

She was shaking her head, her mind a blur. It was as if my words did not register. "I can't. I can't."

"Cannot do what, mate?"

"Protect them. I can't protect them."

Along with her confession, our connection through the collars flooded my mind with anguish and guilt. Danika's emotions swelled inside me to eclipse any pain I'd been feeling on my own. I wished, in that moment, that I was connected to her mind as I was to Varin's so I could know what she was thinking about. Remembering. What she was afraid of. I would destroy worlds for her, yet she gave me no enemy to fight. No target for my protective rage.

I was helpless.

Helpless as I'd been when they tortured Varin. Helpless as I'd been when they'd ravaged his mind by torturing me.

I did not care for the feeling, never wanted to feel this way again. I needed to protect my mate more than I needed air to breathe or blood in my veins.

"This is not acceptable."

"I'm sorry. I don't know what happened. I'm fine. You can put me down now." The chaos of her mind remained unsettled. Her body had not relaxed, her breathing ragged and irregular. She clutched at her chest as if her heart struggled to beat. Tears flowed down her cheeks, yet she seemed completely unaware of their existence. Her eyes remained closed tightly, as if she never wanted to open them again.

"You are lying to me, mate. You are suffering."

"I'm sorry." She took a slow, deep breath. Let it out. Again. Opened her eyes and tried to smile at me. The effort was courageous but pathetic. She was terrified. Hurting.

And she *apologized to me?*

I needed somewhere to take her, somewhere that would calm her. Soothe her.

"I will take you back to our quarters."

"No." Her sudden outburst made me pause and look down into her face. There was that false smile again. "Just put me down. I'll be fine in a few minutes. I promise."

"I can feel you. Do not forget."

"I just...no walls. I can't feel closed in. I need space, that's all." Her gaze moved from my face to the ceiling. She shuddered.

Crippling anxiety wrapped itself around my heart and lungs, squeezing until I struggled to remain calm as it seemed the walls of the corridor were shrinking, closing in on us. In vain I shook my head, tried to clear the sensation. This dread was not mine, but hers.

"No walls." Fuck. The Colony base was domed, completely closed in. The outside atmosphere was not hospitable to long-term exposure, and I doubted a tiny human female would survive even a minute exposed on the surface.

For the first time since we'd arrived on The Colony, I reached for Varin with my mind. I'd been trying to block him out, minimize his pain, but our mate was more important than either of us.

Varin!

His thoughts merged with mine at once, the feeling both odd and all too familiar. *What is wrong with Danika?*

I do not know. She is panicked. Feels as if the walls are closing in on her. Where can I take her?

A busy feeling followed by a buzzing in my ears let me know Varin was speaking with someone. He was probably still in medical. Perhaps I should take Danika there. If nothing else, the doctor could sedate her.

Central garden.

No. I just took her from there.

A pause. More buzzing.

Surnen says there is a star dome. The dome is translucent. I will send directions.

Thank you. The relief I felt was immense. Enduring discomfort, pain, emotional or physical torment was normal for me. I could not bear to feel Danika suffering.

As promised, a clear image of the corridors of the base appeared in my mind thanks to Varin. For once I was grateful for our connection as I turned down a cream-colored corridor and made my way to the only place inside this base where one could look out at countless planets and stars.

The room was not large. A sunken oval in the center was filled with piles of padded seating and soft cushions. Around the edges of the room, small alcoves jutted out, away from the center. Each alcove contained a large chair designed to recline. The center oval was large enough to hold perhaps twenty warriors seated on the built-in bench that lined the outside edge. The cushions were a mix of colors but looked soft and inviting scattered all over the benches and the floor. Around the edge of the dome walls small, recessed lights provided just enough illumination so one would not trip while finding a seat. I had no idea what time of day, or on what dates, The Colony would be under the direct light of the nearest star. Right now the room was dark and silent, the pinpoints of light out in deep space clearly visible through the translucent, dome-shaped walls and ceiling. The place was eerily quiet. Exposed. Ethereal.

There were no walls closing in on us. Not here. In fact, it felt like, if I jumped high enough, we would both float away into space.

"It's beautiful." Danika was still shivering, but her eyes were open and the panic I'd been feeling from her faded to nervous embarrassment. "Thank you for bringing me here."

"I vowed to care for you and protect you." Irritated that she felt the need to thank me, I tried to hide the emotion, as well as my relief that she seemed to be recovering.

Still holding her against my chest, I stepped down into the sunken oval seating area and settled into a pile of cushions. The space invited one to recline, feet up, and mindlessly drift away with the stars above.

Stretched out, I tucked her neatly along my body, placed her head on my shoulder, and stroked her back, silent for long minutes as we both stared out into space.

From here there was no Hive, no war, no battle or death or torture. There was only peace. Stillness. Solitude. And pain, my constant companion.

The quiet unnerved me, but I held my ground against the Hive implants buzzing in my mind, the emotions threatening to drown me. This was not my moment to give in to personal concerns. My mate needed me to be strong for her, therefore, I would be unbreakable.

Patience was a weapon I had learned to wield many times over during our captivity. I utilized the skill now as I waited for my mate to open herself to me. We had asked questions, demanded answers. That strategy had proven unsuccessful. So I waited. Held her without making demands. And was rewarded.

"My dad died when I was eight." She shuddered and her fingertips tapped out a scattered, anxious rhythm on my chest. "He was a good dad. He took care of us and took us camping. We used to make s'mores every weekend even if it was just in the fireplace we had at home."

Tears soaked my uniform beneath her cheek. Still, I remained silent. Waited.

"We didn't have a lot of money, you know? And when my dad passed, it was just my mom and me. I was young, but I knew my mom was struggling. Some nights there was nothing for dinner. I'd sneak over to the neighbor's house, and she would always make me a sandwich. She was in her eighties and her kids had all moved away. She looked out for me."

Danika inhaled and held the breath for overly long, the sound of her exhale loud and ominous, like she was bracing herself.

"My mom was desperate, you know. So, when she got a new boyfriend and he asked her to marry him, she said yes right away. It was fast, like four months. Next thing I know, I have a stepfather and a new baby brother on the way."

That sounded all right to me, but I knew there was more to this story. I stroked my mate's back and sent calm to her through the collars. Strength. She was not alone, and I needed her to feel me.

"After Josh was born, everything changed." She shifted. Sniffed. Wiped her eyes. "Martin didn't like how much time Mom was spending taking care of the baby. He cheated on my mom with a woman he worked with. Which sent my mom into a spiral because we were still poor. We needed him to keep a roof over our heads. She was hurt and confronted him. He denied it, but after that, he got mean. He started drinking. He was in a car accident and had his license taken away. He was hurt, too, and started taking painkillers after the accident. Next thing I know, I'm thirteen, my stepfather is a full-on drug addict, he and Mom are drinking all our money away, my mother is barely coming out of her room, and I'm taking care of the house and my little brother."

"That is not how things should be." I was more than ready to travel to Earth and destroy both humans for causing my mate so much pain. I noticed, too, the more formal term she used for her mother, as if she needed the emotional distance or considered her *mom* and her *mother* to be two different people.

"Tell me about it. I know. I made it work because I loved Josh. He was so little and adorable, and he loved me like crazy. I always made sure he had food, even if I had to lie to my mother. I hid the things I knew he would need. Hid money, too. But Martin found it, and that's when things got really bad."

She stopped speaking, and I bit my tongue, ready to demand she continue. The collars connected us, and I felt the pain building inside her mind. The despair. Regret. A darkness weighed on her mind and her heart. I would not force her to walk in that dark place, not for me.

"Martin found the things I'd kept for Josh. He went crazy. He was jealous of his own son, again. Started beating him first. When I stepped between them, he would hit me. Then he would find my mother and scream at her for turning his kids against him. On the worst nights, I would take my brother into the basement and we would crawl inside a closet. He would sit on my lap, and I would hold him while we listened to them scream and fight each other."

Her hand curled into a fist atop my chest and I half expected her to strike out, but she held very still.

"He got worse and worse. By the time Josh was eight, I knew we wouldn't survive much longer. And my mother was so lost in her own depression and addiction that she didn't have the strength to help us. She was broken, fighting her own demons. I know that now. I hated her for a long time, but sitting in prison gave me a lot of time to think."

Years. My mate had spent years in a human prison for killing another human. Now I feared I understood. "You killed Martin to protect your family."

The sound she made was half groan, half sob. "I did it for Josh. Not for me or for my mom. We were already a lost cause. I flunked out of school. I was trying to work to buy food, but I couldn't leave Josh home alone at night. I knew Martin would kill him eventually. I knew it. He got more and more violent every time."

"So you did what you had to do to protect your brother."

"It was Sunday. I worked a shift at the restaurant on Sunday mornings, good tips for breakfast after everyone gets out of church."

"What is church?"

"It's a place some humans go to practice their religion. While I was at work, my mother called me. She was babbling and crying and I couldn't understand a word she said. I heard Martin yelling at her and Josh screaming at him. I went home as fast as I could."

"You are very brave, mate. And very strong."

She was shaking her head, her disagreement clear through our collars.

"By the time I got home, Martin was passed out in his stupid recliner. Drunk. High. I don't know. But he was out of it." She shuddered. "I went looking for my mom. She was on the floor in her bedroom, foam in her mouth. I checked for a pulse, but...she was gone. Overdosed on something. I kept quiet and went looking for Josh. He was in the closet, curled into a ball, crying. He was eight. Eight years old. I pulled him out of there and I snapped. I couldn't take any more."

Her emotions went cold, numb. I felt her body's warmth next to me, but her mind had gone somewhere dark and empty. I knew that place, had been there many times myself. Numb. Detached. Distanced from what I should have been feeling. I recognized the need to become unfeeling. Efficient. A machine.

"I knew our neighbor had a shotgun, so I took Josh over there and made up some excuse. I don't even remember the lie I told, but it worked. When I knew she was busy getting him something to eat, I stole the gun and a couple of shells. I went home. Martin hadn't moved. I knew if I let him live, my brother and I would be put in his care. I thought my mom was dead. So I put the end of the shotgun right in front of his heart and I—"

"Hush. You do not need to relive this—"

"I killed him."

"How old were you?"

"Seventeen. But they tried me as an adult."

"I do not understand."

"I had to stand trial for murder even though, legally, I was still a kid. I went to prison, and Josh went into the foster care system. He ended up being adopted a couple years later."

The blank emptiness was gone, replaced by loss. Regret. Grief. "You love Josh still. When did you see him last?"

"I didn't see him at all, for years. But I had my attorney keep tabs on him for me. So, I knew when he got adopted and how he was doing. When he turned eighteen, he came to see me." A hot stab of love mixed with loss filled me as she spoke of him. "He wanted to thank me. He remembered everything, you know? He thanked me for killing Martin and feeding him and taking care of him. He told me he loved me."

Great heaving sobs racked her body.

"Why did you not volunteer to be a bride earlier? Why did you wait so long? You could have been with a warrior, protected and cherished, as you should have been your entire life."

She was shaking her head. "No. I couldn't leave until I knew Josh was going to be okay. He's going to college, right now. He's a freshman. And he's got a really good scholarship. He's smart. He told me he's going to go to law school so he can help kids like us. He's going to be okay. I had the Interstellar Brides Program give my money to him, for college."

"You are on another world, and still you provide for him. Protect him. You are a female of worth."

My final words caused her to weep uncontrollably, her mental anguish a storm of chaos I had to ride out with no hope of understanding. Her emotions moved with lightning speed through the collars, flashing from sorrow to rage to love to regret to hope. Her heart was exploding with a lifetime's worth of repressed emotions.

She was safe with me. Nothing would harm her, touch her, threaten her. "Nothing will ever hurt you again, mate. I give you my word."

That caused a flash of anger, directed toward me. Her anger faded almost instantly to despair. Sadness. "What about watching you die? I can't do that, Thomar. I can't."

Fuck. She was right. "I should not have allowed you to become emotionally attached to me. I am sorry. I should have maintained my distance and allowed Varin to fuck you, hold you, be with you. I should have asked the doctor to keep me sedated until it was time for the claiming ceremony."

"Damn it. That's not what I meant." She did strike me with her fist on the chest. Immediately after, she moaned my name and reached to place her palm against my cheek in a very feminine caress. "I tried not to fall in love with you, but it didn't work. I want every minute I can get, Thomar. Every second."

"My death will cause you pain. This is not acceptable."

"It's not your choice, is it?" She rubbed her small thumb along my cheekbone with a gentleness I'd never felt from any other. My chest ached with a pain I did not recognize.

"It's love, Thomar. That pain in your chest, it's love. Trust me. I know how much love can hurt."

Well, fuck. She was correct. She was mine, my perfect mate. Was it any wonder that I had grown to love her already? That just a few days with her would cause me to bond to her? I knew, beyond doubt, that I would kill for her, fight for her, die for her. She was everything to me for however long I had left.

We both stilled as we sensed Varin's approach. When the door to the star dome slid open, we did not move as Varin joined us, taking a seat near Danika's feet and then pulling her legs into his lap. Slowly he moved his hands up and down her calves in a soothing motion. "I did not want to intrude."

Danika removed her hand from my cheek and reached for him. He took her outstretched hand at once. "You are part of us, Varin. Part of me. You are always welcome."

Our mate's care caused a cascade of emotions in Varin

as well. Relief. Hope. Fierce protectiveness pounded through my skull. The strength of his feelings for our female rivaled mine and was amplified by the odd connection we shared through the collars.

Danika shivered. "You guys are intense."

"My apologies." Varin reined his emotions in, and I did the same, locking the ache behind my ribs away for later inspection. Varin looked from our mate's tear streaked face to me. I knew he had heard every word of Danika's story, had shared my outrage that our young mate had not been properly protected. That she had suffered and we had not known, not been able to spare her.

Varin agreed. *We will care for her now.*

Indeed.

Aloud he spoke to both of us. "I waited as long as I could. I did not wish to interfere with our mate's healing. But I could not put him off any longer."

"Who?"

"Helion is here. He insists on speaking to us immediately."

The commander of the Intelligence Core was here? For me? "It has not been a week. I clearly instructed Surnen to give me at least a week."

"The doctor has not yet submitted your request." Varin leaned his head back to rest on the rim of the oval and stared out at the stars. The only thing I could feel from him was exhaustion. "He is here for reasons of his own."

"What did he say? What is the bastard doing here?"

"Who is this Helion?" Danika became stiff in my

arms, but Varin stroked his thumb over her wrist as I ran my fingers through her hair. As quickly as she'd stirred, she settled into our touch, calmed by the security of being surrounded and cared for by her mates. For the first time since I'd seen her, touched her, desired her, I truly felt like I belonged to her. Accepted. Trusted. *Chosen.*

Perhaps loved?

The contentment that filled me as I held her was one I had never experienced before, one I could too easily learn to crave as I had begun to crave the female who had just told me her deepest, darkest secrets.

Varin spoke for both of us. His dislike for Dr. Helion was strong.

"Dr. Helion is a Prillon warrior. He is a commander in the Intelligence Core and reports directly to Prime Nial himself. He is the one in charge of gathering intelligence on the Hive's movements, plans, and weapons. He has spies everywhere, on every planet and among every race."

"So why do you hate him so much? I can feel it. You despise him." Danika's curiosity made my heart nearly burst. My strong, intelligent female was herself again, but calmer. More at peace. Because of me. For once I had healed another rather than caused harm.

"His heart is as black as the darkness of intergalactic space. Endless. Infinite. Cold. When I look into his eyes, I see no soul, only analysis. He will sacrifice anything and anyone to achieve his ends."

"That's harsh."

"He is a harsh male," I confirmed Varin's assessment.

"He sounds great. Let's go meet him." Danika pushed

up off my chest and looked into my eyes with a mischievous look I had not seen before. "Has he met Rachel or any of the other Earth women?"

"Yes. One in particular vexes him. She eliminated a Nexus unit and then disappeared with her mate. He's been trying to track them down for a long time."

"Oh, was that Gwen? The ladies were telling me about her in the garden."

"Yes. I read about her time on The Colony as well," Varin mused, still watching the rotation of the stars. "Gwendolyn Fernandez. Human. No one knows why, but Helion believes he can use her to track down the Hive's central command."

Danika scoffed. "Let me guess, he didn't ask nicely and Gwen told him to shove it up his ass?"

An image of a small, very feisty human female saying such things to the hardened doctor came to mind and I chuckled. If there was one male who needed to be mated, it was Helion. But he refused to be matched. Refused to enter the database and find an Interstellar Bride. On one of our many missions together, before Varin and I were captured, Helion said he would take a mate when the war was over.

Which, if history served, would not be for hundreds of years. Perhaps never.

Danika crawled off my body, and I missed her at once, barely restrained the need to pull her back to me. She stood before us and held out one hand to Varin and one to me. "Come on, gentlemen. Let's go see what this asshole wants."

"You will go back to the safety and privacy of our quarters," I ordered.

"Will not. I'm going with you to meet Helion. He's not ordering you two to do anything without going through me."

I looked from Danika's determined expression to Varin's shocked one as he took her outstretched hand in his own. "You are *very* much like Lady Rone."

She was indeed, and I was not amused. "He is dangerous."

"Are you saying he would hurt me? A woman?"

"No. Never. He is a Prillon warrior of worth."

"Great. Then let's go."

Unwilling, or perhaps unable to deny her anything, I placed my hand in hers and stood. Varin and I'd had many dealings with the infamous Dr. Helion over the years. None of them enjoyable. I doubted this would be any different.

9

Danika

How I had gone from an ass kicking anxiety attack in that garden to complete relaxation. Comfort. Contentment. I was with my mates and I had never felt safer or more at peace than with Varin and Thomar holding me between them like this. The stars shined down into the darkness of the room like tiny fairies sparkling in the blackness of deep space. The moment felt magical and surreal. This wasn't what my life was like, at least not until now.

I settled into the quiet with my mates and they must have sensed my longing to remain for they made no attempt to move or leave the space.

With my cheek pressed to Thomar's chest, I listened to the steady beat of his heart. Slow. Calm.

Something stirred in the back of my mind, a sensation I had felt before but never quite been able to name.

Voices. I heard voices inside my head. And they weren't mine or my mates or anyone's I recognized. Dozens of them.

Screaming. Crying. Begging for help.

In English.

Holy shit.

I bolted into a sitting position, Thomar and Varin both tense and ready to fight.

"What is it mate?" Thomar slipped his feet to the floor and moved to place his body between me and the door as Varin did the same, blocking all access to me from the back of the room.

"Not now." Varin's eyes narrowed as a blade of pain stuck me through our collars.

"Gods." Thomar shook and I knew he felt even more pain than Varin did. Still, he remained in place, protecting me. But from what?

"Do you hear them?" I asked, massaging my temples. I remained seated between the two hulking males. Nothing was getting near me, I was confident in my mates' protection. But the threat wasn't coming from somewhere outside, but from inside my own mind.

"Hear who?" Varin scanned the area behind him. Apparently satisfied there was no threat, he knelt at my feet and looked into my eyes as Thomar remained on guard, watching the door. "Who do you hear? Who is hurting you?"

A blood curdling scream sounded directly behind me. I turned so quickly I lost my balance, Varin's hold the only thing that kept me from falling to the floor.

Less than a second later something stabbed into my

thigh. Something huge, like a knitting needle looking for a vein.

"No. Please, stop. I'll do it. Anything you want. Please!"

The woman's voice was frantic. Panicked. In pain.

"Did you hear that?" I looked into Varin's jewel toned eyes and prayed he wouldn't think I was crazy. Maybe I was. I honestly didn't know. I'd heard cries like this before, in prison, when someone was being punished or broken by the others.

Varin lifted a hand to my cheek and I leaned into his gentle strength. "I hear nothing, mate, only the constant buzz of the Hive implants and Thomar's pain."

"But, the women? Can't you hear them?"

"No. I hear nothing. We will take you to medical at once."

"No." I turned to look up at Thomar, reached for his hand. I tugged until he turned around to look at me. "Can you hear them?"

"I hear many things, mate, but no females."

The woman screamed again, this time the knife-like pain was moving through my lower abdomen, the pain similar to the nightmare cramps I'd had when I was a teenager on my monthly cycle.

Dizzy, I tumbled into Varin's arms, still holding Thomar's hand. "They're doing something to her."

Searing fire, sharp, like a blade cutting me open.

I screamed.

From what seemed like a million miles away, I heard Thomar's voice calling for a medical team.

Sobbing now, I cried as she cried, this mystery woman

inside my mind. I could hear others as well, fighting and howling with rage.

"Hold on, mate. Help is coming." Thomar knelt next to me as well. It was as if I were in two places at once, with my mates and with this woman, a human woman. She was being tortured. Experimented on. And there were others. Watching. Fighting. Desperate.

"Oh, god. Prisoners. They're prisoners."

Huge hands ripped open the woman's abdomen and she arched up off whatever table they had strapped her to. I did as well, my body going stiff, sweat dripping from my brow into my eyes.

Her baby. They were taking her baby.

The Hive.

"No." I shook my head, both me and the woman I was somehow linked to speaking as one. "No-no-no-no—"

She lifted her head and I saw what she did. A baby girl. Beautiful. Perfect.

Integrated.

The Hive doctor, or whatever he was, leaned over to speak to her. His face was blue and silver, eyes black like a shark's. The woman shuddered in repulsion and terror. I felt the scream bubbling up inside her, but she refused to let it out. Somehow she knew the thing—the creature— looming over her would be unaffected. Cold. Robotic in its efficiency. It would sedate her and she wanted to watch, try to see where they were taking her baby.

"We will care for the child. You will sleep now. You will heal."

"No." She protested and I knew she meant it. She

didn't want to live. She knew they—it—the creature--was going to do it to her again. And again.

Like the others.

Her thought, not mine.

What others? What the hell was I seeing? Was this some demented hallucination?

Her vision went black and I came back to myself slowly to find Doctor Surnen kneeling on the floor next to me. Thomar stood behind his left shoulder, Varin behind his right. I was lying on the bench we'd been cuddling on not long ago with the doctor running his scanners over me. An additional male in green was speaking to someone I could not see, and Rachel was leaning over me from above. She had to be on her knees, looking over the edge from the floor the surrounded the sunken seating area. Her dark hair hung down around her face like a frame. "It's okay, Danika. I promise, you're okay."

I was sobbing. Hysterical. Had no memory of how I got in this position or of what had happened to my body in the last few minutes.

But as the woman faded, so did the panic and the pain.

"Thomar? Varin?" I felt bereft. Alone. Where were they? Why weren't they touching me.

"We are here." Relief flooded me as Varin's voice came from the bench above my head and I found him settled there watching me.

I tried to sit up, look for Thomar, but Doctor Surnen placed a hand on my shoulder and pushed me back down. "Do not move."

Thomar placed a heavy hand on the doctor's shoulder. "Careful, doctor. You are addressing my mate."

"Yes, yes." The doctor was clearly unimpressed by Thomar's presence, too absorbed in whatever gadget he was reading to argue.

Something heavy rested on my chest, right on top of my collar bone. I reached for it, but the doctor grabbed my wrist before grabbed hold. "Do not touch that, Danika. Please."

"What is it?" I asked. Rachel stretched down to me with an open hand and I reached for her, more than happy for the friendly squeeze she offered.

Rachel answered before the doctor could. "A Hive frequency jammer."

"What?"

"A frequency jammer. It's the only thing that brought you out of your trance."

"I wasn't in a trance."

Everyone froze. Thomar. Varin. Rachel. The doctor and the medical assistant. Even Governor Maxim, Rachel's mate, appeared from somewhere. He froze too, looking at me. In his hand was a comm, and on that comm screen was the face of another Prillon I didn't recognize.

Thomar's voice was gentle, as if afraid he would startle me. "You were in some kind of trance for nearly two hours, love."

"What? No. I was gone for a few minutes. Just long enough for them to take—" The baby. A moan escaped me as the woman's anguish crushed my chest with remembered grief.

"Them? Who? What did they take?"

"That blue and silver thing with black eyes. He was cutting a baby out of a woman's stomach. He took it—" I looked up at Rachel, who was the only female in the room. "It was a girl. He cut her open and took the baby girl."

Governor Maxim held the comm screen so I could see the face of the Prillon he was speaking to. He must have been listening as well because he cleared his throat. "Surnen, did she say blue and silver? Black eyes?"

"I can speak for myself. And yes. It was dark blue and had black eyes. Not shiny though." I glanced up at Rachel, the only Earth girl here who would understand my reference. "Like a shark's."

Rachel paled and lifted her face to her mate, the governor. "Maxim, she saw a Nexus unit. Gwen said they had eyes like that. So did CJ."

"What's a Nexus unit?" I asked.

Thomar's terror hit me through the collars and my body flooded with adrenaline. I flushed, suddenly overheated. It was hard to breathe. He wasn't afraid for himself. He was terrified for me.

"Calm yourself, Thomar. You are causing your mate distress." The calm reprimand from the doctor affected Thomar immediately and the chaos coming through my collar faded.

Varin had locked his emotions down under ice. Cold. Calm. I had nothing from him. It was like we weren't even connected. "Varin?" I'd rather have rage or fear than nothing.

"I am here." His hand rested on my shoulder and he pressed down a bit so the weight of him anchored me.

The Prillon on the screen spoke to Doctor Surnen again. "What is going on there, Surnen?"

The doctor lifted his scanners from me and stood to take the tablet from the governor. He started to walk away. Thomar grabbed him by the arm and silently shook his head. "No. No secrets."

The voice coming from the screen disagreed. "I am in command here and this is official IC business."

"No, Doctor Helion. It's not. Danika is mine and Varin's business. Anything said will be said to all three of us."

"Fine. Doctor Surnen. Please?"

I was not fond of the arrogant sounding voice on the other side of the call, and I didn't know what the IC was, but I had a feeling I didn't want to know. This Helion jerk did not give me warm fuzzies.

Doctor Surnen cleared his throat and turned back around to face me. I sat slowly, Varin's arm behind my back, and swung my feet over the edge so I didn't feel so helpless and weak.

"Go ahead, doc," I said.

"Your collar is the problem, my lady."

"How is that possible?" Thomar asked.

"Somehow, Danika's mating collar has begun to take on the same characteristics as yours and Varin's. The material has formed a psychic bond with her mind, as it should, but it did not stop the linking process when it should have. There are now tendrils inside her neck and spine that have grown and integrated with her brain tissue. The collar cannot be safely removed."

"What!" Thomar looked like he was going to strangle the doctor. "Why did you not tell me that placing a mating collar on her was dangerous?"

"I did not know. I have never seen anything like this."

I did not care about taking off the stupid collar. I wanted my mating collar to stay exactly where it was, connecting me to my mates. These guys were totally missing the point and I wanted to strangle all of them. "Can we get back to the important thing here?"

The males all stopped and looked at me as if I had two heads. Even Helion, on the comm screen, looked annoyed that I had interrupted.

Thomar scowled. "Nothing is more important than you, female."

"Wrong." I knew he meant what he said. I could feel his absolute conviction through our link. "That thing has an entire prison full of women. He's forcing them to have babies, cutting the infants out of their bodies and then doing it over and over and over again."

"Oh, god." Rachel looked like she was going to vomit, which was pretty much exactly how I was feeling. She looked at the governor. "Like CJ's twins. That Nexus unit tried to take them. Remember?"

The large Prillon motioned for Rachel to come to his side and she did so at once. He wrapped an arm around her and she melted into him, accepting the comfort. I knew exactly how she felt because Varin's strong body was the only thing holding me upright.

Those adorable twins. "CJ and RJ? A Nexus unit tried to take them, too?"

"Yes." Rachel nodded. "She was newly pregnant and the Hive took her to an underground lab and were going to do experiments on them."

Oh shit. "Why? What are they doing?"

"We don't know."

Doctor Helion sighed like we'd just killed his favorite puppy. "I will be there in a few hours with a strike team. Keep her sedated. We can't afford to lose her to the Hive mind before we locate the prisoners."

"I'm right here, you know." Jerk talking about me like I was an object and not a real, living, breathing human being sitting here listening to every word.

My irritation did nothing to affect him as the screen was already blank. I looked from the screen to Doctor Surnen and shook my head. "You try to stick a needle in me and it'll be the last thing you ever do." I meant it.

Thomar moved to stand between me and the doctor. "You heard my mate. No sedative. I don't care what Helion said."

"Agreed. We just got you out of a near comatose state, my lady. We do not want to risk sending you there again." He grinned at me then and now that I was used to looking at these Prillon warrior hotties, I had to admit he was kinda gorgeous. Not as sexy as my mates, but still. Not bad at all. Mikki was lucky to have him.

Mikki. There was a human woman I hadn't met yet. According to Rachel, she was off collecting samples or something with a science team. These ladies on The

Colony were all amazing and I was...just me. Totally not amazing at anything except surviving.

I reached for Thomar and wrapped my hand around his forearm. He moved to my side instantly, just as I'd known he would. He thought he was a big, mean brute. He was just a giant teddy bear. Not that I'd tell him that. Varin was stoic and more in control than Thomar. In fact, Thomar and I both needed our second to anchor our crazy emotions. But I wouldn't tell him that either. The egos on these two mates of mine were big enough already.

10

Thomar, Three Hours Later, Medical Station

$\mathcal{H}$elion, the Prillon commander, doctor, whatever the fuck he was, had better back away from my mate or he was going to be crushed into a bloody pulp.

Danika sat on an exam table in medical as both Doctor Surnen and Doctor Helion scanned, poked, prodded, took blood samples and spoke in medical terms I didn't understand.

Danika didn't protest when I pulled her into my lap and held her through all of it. She was so sensitive to me, so attuned to my needs. If I'd had to watch them hurt her from across the room, I would have lost control.

Gods, if only I wasn't so fucked up. So broken. I was a lost cause. Poison to everything and everyone I touched. First I'd ruined Varin's life. Now I had infected the most beautiful, pure, precious thing I'd ever known. My female. My mate.

Mine.

"Thomar, stop fretting. I'm fine. I'm going to be fine."

Danika tried to reassure me. Failed. The entire situation had me on edge. What the fuck was a Nexus unit doing inside my mate's head? Why was she hearing voices? And why had her collar acted like Hive technology rather than Prillon. The mating collar was standard issue. Mass produced. The same type my people had used for hundreds of years. It should have been safe.

Instead of safety from her mates, our female had Hive integrations infiltrating her body, her skull. Her vision and hearing and pain sensors had been affected. My enemy could strike at her from afar. And I was responsible. The thought made me ill.

I never should have agreed to claim Danika. Never. I should have walked away and ended my life so Varin could find a second and live out the rest of his days in peace with Danika next to him.

I'd been weak. Selfish. Unable to resist indulging myself for a few days, touching her soft skin, fucking her, listening to her cries of pleasure. The rush had been indescribable after so many months of hell. The gentleness of her spirit had been a balm I sorely needed. She loved us now. I knew Varin felt the truth of her emotions through our collars as clearly as I. My death would cause her distress.

Now she would suffer. Varin would suffer. I could have prevented all of this from happening if I'd been strong enough to—

"Damn it, Thomar. I said knock it off. I'm trying to decipher doctor speak and I can't with you moping about in my head." Danika softened her scolding tone by lifting my hand to her lips and planting a kiss on my skin.

"I do not mope."

Danika burst into feminine laughter and I was once again amazed at her resiliency. Her strength. "You do. You're a regular drama king." She smiled at me and squeezed my hand. Of course, I pulled her closer to me at once.

"Think happy thoughts, okay?"

"I am not happy. This situation is not acceptable. You will not be going anywhere with the strike team."

"I'm going. And so are you."

"No. You will remain here. Safe."

"I'm going. You can stay here if you want to. Your choice." She looked around for our second. "Where's Varin?"

"I do not know." He had disappeared somewhere along the way from the star dome to the medical station.

As if on cue, the medical station doors slid open and Varin walked in, his arms loaded with weapons and gear. "This should be everything we need."

Doctor Helion, who, until this point, had said no more than a handful of words since his arrival on The Colony, looked at Varin and scowled. "Where did you acquire those weapons?"

Varin raised a brow and crossed his arms across his chest. "I made them."

"Those are not standard issue."

Varin snorted in disgust. "Of course not."

Moving slowly, I stood and gently placed Danika on the medical bed so I could approach Varin. He reached down and tossed me our favorite battle armor and an ion rifle that would take out a charging Atlan with one shot. This gear was the reason we'd been able to break free from the Hive base. We'd been the Hive's prisoners, but we'd been learning, too. Watching. Studying.

I grabbed the rifle out of the air and moved it behind me, out of reach, when Helion made a grab for it.

"There was no mention of these weapons or armor adaptations in your debriefing reports." Helion looked mad as an Atlan in beast mode. Good. Now he knew how I felt about him putting my mate in danger.

"No one asked the right questions and we didn't feel like talking," Varin said.

A smile escaped and I met Varin's gaze in approval. He was a worthy second. Strong enough to care for Danika once I was gone. A powerful ally and closer than a brother. I made sure he knew how I felt. We weren't ones to cry and talk about emotions, but I wanted him to know I loved him, too. Family. He was family and I pushed that knowledge to him through the collars. Hard.

He doubled over and choked. "Enough, Thomar. I know."

"Hand me the weapon. Now. That's an order." Helion stood facing me, clearly not used to being ignored.

"Nope. Not a toy." I stepped back and placed the rifle on the med counter behind me as I stripped and changed into my armor. "And I don't take orders from you. You don't outrank me, Commander."

"Fuck. Hard-headed Arcas family."

That made Danika burst into laughter and I grinned back at her, feeling almost normal for the first time since before I'd been captured by the Hive. I would have no issue sharing what Varin and I had learned during our captivity. Had intended to, in fact. But we'd been distracted by a small, beautiful, sexy female to care for. To touch. To fuck. She was a thousand times more interesting than the rifle behind me.

Love poured into me. Pure. Aching. Perfect. Unable to stop myself, I walked across the room and took Danika's face between my hands. I stared down into her eyes and let everything I was feeling pour into her. Longing. Gratitude. Respect. Love. Desire. Need. She was everything to me. Everything.

"Thomar." My name was barely a whisper on her lips as I leaned down and took her mouth, not caring who witnessed my need for this female.

Behind me I heard Varin reproach Helion. "Don't think so, doc."

I kissed my mate, confident Varin could handle the Intelligence Core commander.

"You do not outrank me, Varin Mordin. You will follow my orders and give me that weapon for inspection."

"I have direct orders from Commander Arcas *not* to allow anyone to touch these weapons."

"Gods be damned." I felt Helion's eyes burning into the back of my skull.

Danika was grinning as I ended the kiss and rested my forehead against hers. Holding her. Loving her. "He's glaring at me, isn't he?"

She leaned around my shoulder to take a peek. "Yep." Her smile melted me. She owned me.

I kissed her once more on the lips, quickly, then joined Varin and finished putting on our customized armor. Rifle attached to my back, I looked over Varin's gear as he checked mine. When we were both satisfied we turned as one to face the doctors, our mate, and the governor and his female who had been sitting quietly off to the side the entire time. Silent. Watching. Waiting.

My pain levels had been lower than usual for several hours. I attributed the change to my connection to Danika, but as I stood waiting to hear what Helion's plan of attack would be, the buzzing agony rushed over me like a flood.

Danika cried out and put her hands up to her temples. "God, they're so loud."

Voices. The buzzing in my head, all this time, had been voices? Crying for help. Screaming in pain. Begging to go home.

Fuck. I could hear them now. The females. Crying.

Helion rushed to stand before her. "What are they saying?"

"I don't know." Danika moaned and her face paled. She turned large, pain filled eyes at me. "I'm sorry. I can't make it stop."

"Do not apologize mate." Varin's tone was soft, calm. "We will end your torment. I vow this to you."

Doctor Surnen stepped forward with a ReGen wand and waved it over Danika's head. The action made her pain worse, her agony like a knife spike through our mating collars.

"Stop, doctor. You are hurting her." Varin spoke once more, his tone clearly a threat. Doctor Surnen stepped back at once, clearly appalled that he had caused harm. I focused on staying in control as my own pain amplified until I felt like I had razors running around on a racing track inside my head.

"Give me that." Doctor Helion reached for the ReGen wand and a sedative from a nearby tray. "That's enough. She is a female and she is in pain. She must be sedated."

"No!" Danika was crawling backward, away from Helion. Her agitation pushed me over the edge. No one was going to frighten my mate. Or hurt her. Or force her to do anything she didn't want to do.

This male really wanted to die. I didn't care if I had to kill the fucking Prime himself to protect her. She. Was. Mine.

I blinked and the doctor was hanging, back to the wall, my hand at his throat. He was a Prillon warrior, but I was an Arcas. Royal bloodline. Larger. Stronger. Faster.

Fucking meaner.

"Do not touch her."

Helion lifted his hands to the sides, palms out in surrender. "So, I finally witness the famous Arcas rage."

The growl that came from my throat was more animal than male. Years of taunts and sideways glances pushed at my control. My entire life I'd been treated this way, as a bomb on the verge of exploding. Unstable. Lacking control. Without honor. Never to be trusted around a female. The accumulation of insults and accusations festered in my gut like rotten meat.

This was why I avoided other Prillons. Why I had

volunteered to serve in the Coalition Fleet the moment I'd been old enough. I couldn't accept the arrogant disdain of the other Prillons and all because of a male who'd been dead for several hundred years.

"If I were truly angry, you would be dead."

"Calm down. I would never hurt a female."

I relaxed my hold on his throat but did not set him down. "Do not touch her again. She is mine. I *will* kill you. Do you understand me?"

"Yes, yes. You're worse than an Atlan beast."

That comment earned him another growl.

"Commander Arcas, please. I did not intend to cause your mate harm, only to ease her suffering."

"It's her choice. Leave her alone." Varin stood at my shoulder, as he always had, and stared up at the doctor as well. "I've heard about you, Helion. And none of it was good."

Doctor Helion had no expression on his face as I slowly lowered his feet to the floor. Part of me hoped he would make a move to strike at me, give me an excuse to rip him into pieces. Unfortunately, his control was irrefutable, his face like stone. "If all we're going to do is snarl at one another, I suggest we meet up with my team and get moving. We've tracked the signal affecting you two and your mate. Unfortunately, the signal is moving."

"Seems to be coming from a ship," Doctor Surnen muttered.

"Perhaps." Helion answered him. "We don't know how long we'll have until the Nexus unit realizes he has a mental connection to Danika. And there is no doubt, there is a connection."

Danika's body shivered, her reluctant agreement coming through the collars. She thought Helion was right. Which meant my mate was linked to the most dangerous creature to exist.

Rachel stood. "What happens if the Nexus does figure it out?"

Helion looked at Danika when he answered. "The Hive could block the signal so we lose our ability to track their location. As far as Danika, I do not know."

"I do," Danika said.

Varin moved to our mate and pulled her close. Immediately I felt her relief at the offer of comfort. His compulsion to care for her driving him as it drove me. We were both gone over our female. Lost.

Helion, however, had no interest mates or offering comfort. "What are you not telling me, female?"

"It's just a feeling, like he *wants* me to come to him."

11

Varin, Intelligence Core Strike Ship

expected at least fifty Prillon warriors and half that many Atlans to be in Helion's team. I assumed Governor Maxim would send as many fighters from The Colony as possible.

There were less than a dozen Prillons on Helion's ship. Only two Atlans. Governor Maxim and his second, a brute of a warrior named Ryston came along, but only because their mate, Rachel, insisted on accompanying Doctor Surnen to the Hive installation in case any of the females or infants needed medical attention.

Helion sat waiting for us in a small, brightly lit conference room. There was a table with six chairs. He sat in one. Thomar led Danika to another. Rachel sat next to her and the rest of us stood. One chair would easily have held both human females. They looked so small and delicate, like children swinging their feet far above the floor as Helion rattled off battle strategy, infiltration tactics and what he knew about the prison ship so far.

Which was next to nothing.

He was supposed to be the most informed warrior in the entire Coalition Fleet. To that end, he knew surprisingly little. I found his lack of knowledge irritating, to say the least. Especially when he was placing our mate in danger. Form the scowl on Governor Maxim's face he felt the same.

I knew exactly how Thomar was feeling. He fought the urge to finish what he'd started back on The Colony in that medical station.

The thought made me grin. Seeing Helion hanging by his throat up against the wall had been very enjoyable indeed. Not for the first time, I'd been grateful for Thomar's temper. That fighting spirit had saved our lives more than once. I admired his resolve. He, however, had always seen it as a curse, as had our people. A fact I had yet to forgive.

Danika's feminine fire seeped into my mind like a whirlwind of flame. She was angry about something. But what?

I had no idea. I'd been lost in my own thoughts, not paying attention. A raid was a raid. I'd been on hundreds. Board. Fight. Kill or be killed. The Hive did not vary their fighting style or ferocity. They were efficient, deadly enemies. I didn't need Helion to tell me that.

"Excuse me. What, exactly, is a Nexus unit?" Danika asked. "Because, as far as I can tell, you are taking my mates to a prison ship to fight one of these things, but no one seems to know exactly what it is."

Helion stared at Danika, unblinking. "There is one living being who knows the Nexus inside and out. A human. Gwendolyn Fernandez, matched mate to Makarios of Kronos. Do you know how much of that information she has shared?"

"No."

"None."

"Have you asked nicely? Or do you talk to her like she's an idiot? Kind of like you're talking to me right now?" Danika glared right back and I felt pride and wonder spread through my chest. My tiny female was glaring at one of the most feared Prillon warriors in the Coalition.

Helion sighed and looked up at Thomar. "I suggest you control your female."

Thomar's growl had the Atlan guard that seemed to be within arm's reach of Helion at all times—probably a personal bodyguard—moved toward Thomar.

I stepped between them, blocking the Atlan's path. He was Atlan, but I was integrated with enough Hive tech to rip him to pieces. I would not be easy prey, not even for a beast.

"All of you, knock it off. Put them away." Danika was shaking her head, her palms flat on the table as if that would help her make her point.

"What are you talking about? Put what away?" Rachel asked.

"Their dicks. They've all got 'em out on the table for measuring."

Stunned silence. Not one male in the room could believe the crude accusation that had come from our mate's throat.

Rachel broke the silence with a burst of laughter. "Oh my God. You did *not* just say that."

Danika shrugged. "Fresh out of prison. On our way to another one, this time, in freaking outer space. What can I say? I like to keep it real." She turned from Thomar to glance at me, then the Atlan who had stopped in his tracks. When no one moved, she returned her attention to Helion. "So? Spill. I know you know. I can see it in your face. Word of advice, don't play poker with the ladies in the west wing. They'll clean you out. Your poker face is terrible."

Helion blinked. Slowly. "I do not understand a word you just said."

Rachel took pity on all of us and translated the strange human speak. "She believes you know a lot more about the Nexus unit than you are telling us. She suspects, by the look on your face, that you are lying to all of us and she's calling you out."

The doctor, Helion, turned that cold brown stare from Danika to me. I stared right back. "Well? You heard her? Spill."

Spill. I liked that word. Short. Direct. To the point. A command.

"Very well." Helion leaned back in his chair and nodded to the Atlan, who resumed his position guarding the door. "Nothing revealed here can leave this room without permission from me and me alone."

Danika was moving her hand in a twirling motion,

around and around as if she were trying to encourage Helion to speak faster. The thought of my small, fragile female giving orders to Helion made me want to laugh.

I hoped he would take a mate, and I hoped she would be human. From Earth. Sassy and strong as both Rachel and Danika were proving to be.

"We believe the Nexus units serve as a central link to thousands of minds in the Hive collective. When a Nexus unit is eliminated, every individual linked to that Nexus mind drops dead instantly. Hundreds, sometimes thousands of their Soldiers eliminated."

"Then why are you fighting the regular Hive? Why not just hunt down all these Nexus guys and kill them?" Danika asked.

"We cannot find them. They are protected by the collective. Secretive. Intelligent. They are the master strategists for their troops. The older they are, the more integrated warriors and fighters they have, the deeper they are in the maze of minds. They rarely show themselves. We only recently discovered their existence, within the last few years."

"The war has been raging for hundreds of years." Rachel sounded upset. "How is that possible?"

"They remain hidden. Unseen. Ghosts or phantoms that move from shadow to shadow, mind to mind."

"Then how do you know the one I saw was one of these Nexus units?" Danika asked.

"They are distinct in appearance. Dark blue skin marked with silver and eyes that are black as deep space, but dull, without spark or spirit."

"Like a shark." Danika shuddered. "I hate sharks. They give me the creeps."

"Don't let Mikki hear you say that. She loves 'em," Rachel informed her.

I had no idea what this shark entity might be, but I intended to research the Earth creature as soon as we returned to The Colony.

Helion continued, "Their gaze is hypnotic. If you look them in the eye, they can place you in an instant trance, control your thoughts, make you do anything. Walk off a cliff. Torture your own child. Kill your mate. Anything."

"What?" Danika's shock vibrated through my system and made my heart pound. The collars were great in bed, when everything was hot and sweaty, desire and pleasure. But fear transmitted just as easily. And Danika, despite her stoic outer appearance, was suddenly freezing her emotions in ice. Retreating. Locking everything down tight.

"How do you know this to be true?" Thomar asked and I sensed his disbelief warring with resignation. We were going after this thing. I could feel his determination to do what he could to protect our mate, his people and defeat the Hive. As always, I would be at his side. Thomar would never fight alone, not while I lived.

"We have been working on pieces of a Nexus unit's brain tissue and helmet for a couple of years, developed some brain implants to both mimic and deflect the Nexus unit's influence. A human fighter, a female in fact, chased down a Nexus unit on Latiri 4's moon and teamed up with an Atlan Warlord to bring us his head."

"Whoa. What?" Rachel looked shocked. "A human woman? Why haven't I met her?"

"She was Fleet. Not a bride, and she has since retired. I believe Megan and Warlord Nyko now reside on Atlan. This line of questioning is irrelevant to the current situation." Doctor Helion looked down at a small tablet in the palm of his hand. "You two, Commander Arcas and Captain Varin, and now you as well, Danika, have integrations that are killing you."

What the fuck did he just say?

"Surnen?"

The golden Prillon doctor looked like he'd been beaten. "I didn't want to tell you all until after the mission. I haven't given up hope we can figure something out. But yes. All three of you are linked in a way we don't understand. And all three of you are dying."

I couldn't breathe. Dread moved like a heavy stone from my throat to my feet and I remained rooted in place, unable to respond. Danika was dying? I didn't give a fuck about myself, but not Danika. No.

I expected fear from my little female. Despair. The same level of grief and anger I was feeling. Instead, her emotions were calm. Fatalistic. Resigned and accepting of her fate.

"No. I will not accept this. Kill me now, Doctor. Break the link between us. Free her." I turned to Thomar and he nodded. I turned back to Surnen. "Thomar agrees."

"No!" Danika protested, her tone that of a female more than comfortable scolding her mates. At least we had given her that measure of safety and confidence. It would serve her well when she found another pair of Prillon males.

Doctor Helion was already shaking his head. "I'm afraid that wouldn't make any difference. The programming, contagion, whatever it is that made your collars behave so differently is already in her system. We cannot remove he collar without killing her. We cannot stop the integration from spreading. If you two sacrifice yourselves, her situation will be unaffected."

Fuck. We'd be dead and she'd be alone. This was a nightmare. I'd sacrificed everything to fight in this war. My family had disowned me when I'd chosen to serve as second to a member of the Arcas family. They refused to meet Thomar and judge him for his own merits, the taint of his family name all they were willing to consider. Thomar and I survived countless battles, torture, years of agony and a closeness of mind that would drive most Prillons mad. I had endured out of hope. Hope that we would one day find a mate and become whole again.

Instead, we were killing her.

Years of rage rushed through me in the blink of an eye and I was at the wall, ripping a massive panel free and throwing it to the ground.

"Be calm, Varin. We'll figure this out." Danika was suddenly at my side, her gentle touch on my arm, her mind and emotions nothing but warmth. Contentment. Love. "I love you. We'll figure it out. And if I die, I have no regrets. Do you?"

The vulnerability was there, in her gaze, in her thoughts. I wanted to lie and tell her I would have been better off without her. But I could not. She had saved my soul, made the sacrifices worth the pain. Validated every choice I had ever made simply be being real. Being mine. Ours.

Tears streamed silently from her eyes to race down her cheeks. The rage drained from me and left me emptied of everything but love for her and for Thomar. Fear. I placed both hands on her cheeks and wiped the tears away with my thumbs. Gave her the truth I knew she needed. "I would change nothing."

With a sigh she pressed forward and wrapped her arms around me. I held her tightly as Thomar shuddered with the power of the emotions drowning all three of us. He looked at Helion and once more I admired his strength of will. His power. His control. He was truly an exceptional warrior and the most skilled I'd ever seen. I hadn't chosen to be his second because he was from an ancient bloodline. Nor because we had grown up together, trained together and were closer than brothers. I'd chosen him because no other warrior measured up, including myself.

"How long do we have?" Thomar asked.

"You, maybe a week. Varin," Doctor Surnen looked at me. "Two at most."

"And Danika?" I asked.

This time it was Helion who replied. "We don't know. The integrations continue to infiltrate, duplicate and merge with her brain cells. At the current rate? A few days. Four at most."

"Oh my God." Rachel looked like she was going to faint, her face a pale, sickly yellow.

Four days? We would lose our mate in four days?

Helion interrupted before I could fully process what the doctor had just told us. "The adaptations to your mating collars are unique and something we have never seen before. The Hive does not do anything without a purpose. We need to capture the Nexus unit and find out what they are doing. How to reverse it."

It was that moment, staring at his face, that I knew the truth.

"You don't care about the women or the babies, or us. You just want to get your hands on that Nexus unit."

Danika's soft gasp was a blend of disgust and shock but my mind filled with ice cold rage. Not mine. Not Thomar's.

Hers.

———

Danika

A FIERCE PROTECTIVENESS filled me with rage unlike anything I'd felt since the day—

No. My mates were not helpless, scared little boys like Josh had been. They were warriors. Strong. Scarred. They had survived things I couldn't imagine. Still, the need to make sure my mates were well and cared for had become my new obsession.

And that meant making sure they would be okay even if I wasn't around to see it.

If getting this Nexus thing was their only chance, so be it. But I knew they would not be able to live with themselves if they left defenseless woman and children behind.

Hell, I couldn't live with that, either. I'd proven that once. Killed to protect my brother. I could do it again for babies. Chubby, adorable, helpless babies.

I had no intention of ever having one of my own, but that didn't mean I didn't love the little mess makers. When other people had them, but still. Babies. Who experimented on babies? Abandoned them?

Apparently, Helion had already made the choice to do exactly that if necessary.

If I could have, I would have walked over to Helion and slapped that frigid, unfeeling face until it was bloody. Unfortunately, Varin held me in his arms, refused to let go when I tried to pull away and pounce. Thomar must have felt my intention as well. He caught my eye and shook his head, the movement so small I barely caught it. But I did, so I tried to calm down, despite the fact that I'd just been handed a death sentence by the single largest asshole I'd ever had the displeasure of meeting.

This situation left me no choice. Thomar and Varin were mine and I wasn't giving them up. Not to the Hive implants and not to this Prillon, James Bond wannabe and his less than honorable agenda.

"We save the women and babies first." I turned in Varin's arms and wrapped his arms around my body for comfort, his heat and his strength at my back. I covered his hands with mine so he'd feel me on his flesh as well as in his mind. I was determined. I didn't care if I ended up dying because we didn't go after the Nexus unit first.

Babies were babies. What kind of emotionless troll was this guy?

"Capturing this Nexus unit may very well save millions of females and their children on hundreds of worlds." His gaze was certain. Unmoving. "Would you sacrifice millions to save a few?"

That kind of troll. The rational, pragmatic, ice cold analysis kind. When he put it that way, he made me sound like an irresponsible child.

Gathering my thoughts, I took a moment to answer him. "You do not know what the outcome would be. You are not certain that you cannot do both."

"The odds of a successful mission decrease with additional objectives."

"I don't care. I can't do it. I will not leave women and babies behind. I refuse. You'll just have to find a way to do both."

"I agree." Rachel's frown was severe, her face pink with anger.

Her mates looked at one another and nodded. Maxim spoke. "We are in agreement, Helion. Prillon warriors do not leave females or young ones unprotected. You ask too much."

For once, Helion looked exhausted. Fatalistic. Utterly defeated. "I know. This war asks too much of us all."

"So, are we in agreement?" I asked. "We go in, we free the prisoners *and* we capture this Nexus thing?" I couldn't live with myself if we went in there and left them behind. I'd rather be dead than try to live with leaving babies to die. Or worse. Who knew what the weird blue alien with shark eyes would do with an innocent baby? The thought made me shudder.

"Very well," Helion agreed.

"Where is the Nexus unit now?" Thomar asked. "Can the scanners pinpoint its location on the prison ship?"

A fighter sitting at one of the control stations answered. "We have been tracking your mate's connection to the Nexus unit. We are close enough now that I have scanned the ship. The Nexus in the standard integration bay. I'm also picking up signals for at least two dozen prisoners and several infants in that area."

"I bet those prisoners are all women," I muttered.

"Of course," Varin's response sounded bored, but I could feel the underlying fury.

"How many fighters are on that ship? Guards? Pilots?"

The fighter checked his screens. "Six fighters in the control room, two with the Nexus unit and fifteen appear to be locked into hibernation cells."

"That won't last long," Thomar said. "The moment we hit them those fighters will be activated."

"And at full power," Varin added.

Thomar looked over to Varin, then down at me. Our gazes locked. "You will remain here, on Helion's ship."

"I will not. Those women are going to be scared to death. Who knows if they've ever seen a Prillon or an Atlan before? No way. I'm going. They are going to need a friendly face." And that was only half of the reason.

Thomar locked his gaze to mine. I felt the struggle within him, the need to protect me warring with my logic as well as my need to go with them. Protect them. Make sure they came out of this alive and in one piece, mentally as well as physically.

I stared right back, furious, hurt and determined not to let my mates out of my sight. I knew Helion's type, the smooth, lying, *the-end-justifies-the-means* kind of people. I knew my mates were warriors, first and always. If they believed they needed to die to save me, they'd die. They'd sacrifice themselves. *Again.*

I would not have it. I was going to be dead in four days anyway. Might as well die protecting the only males I'd ever loved. "I know how to fire a gun. I know how to fight. I didn't survive all those years in federal prison being weak. My mates are not going anywhere without me."

The connection to my mates through my collar was surprisingly quiet. I wasn't sure what that meant, but I was too busy staring down first Thomar, then Maxim and finally, Helion, to worry about the eerie calm at the moment.

The silence stretched. I did not budge. I couldn't risk losing them. Even better, I knew, *knew,* that if Helion tried to lay a hand on me he'd be dead before he realized he'd made a mistake. Thomar moved slightly, angled his body just enough to partially block my body from Helion's view. Varin had my back. I stared down a huge, battle-hardened, probably psychopathic alien warrior and for the first time in my life, I felt no fear for my personal safety. None. I felt truly and completely safe.

"Very well." Helion turned to the fighter at the control panel. "How long do we have?"

"One hundred thirty-seven minutes to attack position."

Helion stood. "I suggest everyone get something to eat. Rest. Check your gear. You know the routine. Be in the launch bay in one-oh-seven."

I'd won an argument for one of the first times in my life. And with a mean Prillon secret agent. The small victory made dizzy, and it made me bold. Drunk. Reckless. I only had four days. Maybe, I only had one hundred and seven minutes. "Everyone out. Get out of here. I need to talk to my mates. *Alone.*"

12

Danika

The door slid closed behind the last of the meeting attendees. I followed him out and I placed my hand over the sensor I knew would lock the door. Turning to face my mates, I rubbed my upper arms with my hands, suddenly cold. "I don't like that guy."

When my mates still didn't say anything, I tried to stop shivering and looked at them each in turn. They stared back and the link between our mating collars remained...empty. "What?" I glanced from Thomar to Varin and back again with growing alarm. Had I made them angry? "What's wrong? Why aren't you saying anything?"

Thomar spoke first. "No one has ever tried to protect us before."

I waved my hand in the air. That was ridiculous and

wrong. And I didn't believe them. With all the missions they'd been on? No way.

Varin rose from his seat slowly, every move carefully controlled. "You are small, Danika. Female. We protect you. There is no need to protect us, mate. No need to challenge one as ruthless and powerful as Helion."

I felt something from Varin, finally. Concern. *Shock.*

Lust. A need so strong it nearly strangled me and I wrapped my arms around my stomach in an effort to ground myself. To think beyond the wetness growing between my legs, the drumbeat of my suddenly throbbing core.

"You two have been in battle. Right? Didn't you have a team with you that had your backs?"

"Never. I am an Arcas. Varin allied himself to me. We did not serve on a team with other warriors. We fight alone." Thomar's blunt response stunned me. That made no sense.

"I don't understand. I know you said your family was cursed or something, but that sounds like they just sent you two out to die."

"Many times." Varin's affirmation was stoic. Accepting.

"That's bullshit. You two need protecting. Sorry, but it's true. They ask you to throw yourselves on a spike and you would. All you big, hulking warrior types are that way. I know. Soldiers on Earth are the same, thinking they have to save everyone all the time."

"We are not human," Varin argued while Thomar watched me with eyes that burned through the dress I'd generated for myself. I could *feel* his gaze like a hot caress.

"I am. I'm human and flawed and scared and stubborn. I'm also in love with both of you and I'm not letting you go. I protect the people I love. It's kinda my thing." Feeling a bit more in control, I put my hands on my hips and stared at the most beautiful, honorable, courageous males I'd ever met. "You are never fighting alone again. Not while I'm alive. I am going to protect you because you obviously won't protect yourselves. You'll get used to it."

My mates continued to stare at me. Stunned. They could not see themselves as I did, so I concentrated my thoughts and emotions and shoved them through the collar the best I could. I wanted them to feel what I felt when I looked at them, needed them to know how they affected me. I shuffled through the emotions one by one, focused on each thought, each feeling until the collars resonated with their understanding before moving on to the next.

Safe. I felt safe. Loved. Protected. Cherished. Desired. But that was not all. I loved them, their honor and grumbling and courage. Their loyalty to their people. Their strength in surviving the Hive and their torture. I loved the way they touched me. Kissed me. Craved me. Needed to be near me. I loved that I was an anchor in their minds, their purpose and their reason for fighting. I loved the strange designs on their skin, the way they tasted, the way I felt when I was between them, surrounded by them.

I'd come from a dark place, a hopeless place. I suspected they had as well. I could not go back there and survive. My mind would fracture, I could feel the cracks sometimes when I thought about losing Thomar, the grief of losing my father, my real father, would rise up like a storm and torment me with the agony and despair I knew would strike if I lost either one of my mates. And now, knowing Varin would be right behind him?

No. I could not accept that.

So I would not lose them. Not Varin, with his stoic loyalty and seemingly unending sacrifice as he took Thomar's pain. Not Thomar with his mind splintered into pieces, each sliver screaming in agony, surrounded by suffering voices he could not deny. They were good to their cores, honorable and courageous and perfect.

And they were *mine*.

"Helion cannot have you. Do you understand me?" I had become a bossy, bitchy, nagging wife and I didn't care. This was important. *They* were important. "You. Are. Mine. Not his. Mine."

We stood, me at the door, Thomar on the opposite side of the table, Varin on the near side. I moved slowly as they seemed poised to shatter. Or pounce.

When I stood at the head of the table, equidistant between them, I rested by hands on top of the empty chair back and sighed. "Are you two going to say something? You are behaving strangely and I don't know if you are angry with me, or—"

"Fuck." Thomar moved so quickly I was pressed to the wall, his mouth on mine before I could blink.

His kiss devoured me. I could not think, only feel.

Like a damn had broken, both of my mates seemed to have lost control. Their emotions were a blurry chaos of lust. Fear for me. Need.

Varin appeared at my side. "We need you."

"Yes. Do it now." I was already soaking wet, more than

ready for a hard cock to sink deep. Make me feel. Make me forget this horrible ship and this insane mission.

Varin knelt at my feet and pulled my dress up slowly, sliding his palms over my legs and thighs, my ass as he pulled my new panties down around my ankles. I did not need to step out of them. Thomar has his cock free form his pants.

He lifted me, pressed my back to the wall of the meeting room and thrust deep.

He fucked me then, fast. Without mercy. I came in moments, my cries of pleasure stolen from the air as Varin turned my face to him and slammed his mouth down on mind.

Thomar froze in place as my pussy pulsed around him, as Varin kissed me, his hand rubbing the soft mounds of my ass. He slipped a finger inside and I groaned, eager for more. I needed more. Both of them. Fucking me. Filling me up. We'd been playing with the alien device in my ass for the last few days. I was ready. More than ready.

"I need you, Danika. I need you." Varin's plea was rough against my lips, his voice ragged, as if the admission had been violently torn form his throat.

"Yes. I want you both. I need you, too." I did not want to die without knowing what it was to be truly between them, claimed. One with both of my mates.

Thomar spun around so that his back was to the wall. His cock remained buried deep as aftershocks pulsed through my body.

Varin position himself behind me and I felt the warmth of the lubrication coating my ass, grateful for alien technology that made this possible. I didn't want to wait. I was terrified of losing one of them. Of losing myself on that prison ship.

Thomar lifted and lowered me on his cock several times as Varin inserted first one finger, then two into my ass. The sensation of being invaded, the friction drove my desire high once more. When I was panting and desperate, Varin positioned himself behind me, the head of his cock exactly where I wanted it. Needed it.

"Are you ready?"

"Yes. I want you both. I love you. I love both of you."

Thomar's emotions were raw with a new pain, one I recognized.

It hurt to be loved the first time. Years of suffering, of emptiness, of believing he was not worthy of love moved through him—and me—like someone ripping a bandage off an unhealed wound.

"Thomar." His name was a whimper in my throat and I lifted my mouth to his, drank him down as Varin pressed into me from behind, made us one.

His cock was huge, the pressure uncomfortable at first. With a popping sensation, he slid deep and I cried out. So full. So shockingly full of my mates. I'd never felt so owned. Claimed. Taken.

Home. They felt like home.

Varin's hands came around to fondle and caress my breasts through my dress. Thomar's mouth met mine once more and they moved. Slowly. Carefully. Like I was precious and perfect and breakable.

I had not allowed myself to be weak since my father died. I couldn't. Weakness meant more abuse, more fighting, more pain. But now, between them, my control shattered and I sobbed, the emotions pouring through me too strong to be contained in my small, human body.

I kissed Thomar, held onto him, buried my fingers in his hair. I welcomed Varin, thrust my sensitive nipples into his hands, squeezed both of my mates with my inner muscles. Claimed them as they were claiming me. All as tears streamed down my face like a river.

The orgasm came for all of us at once, an explosion in three shared minds. Varin's mouth settled over my shoulder as he pumped his seed into my ass, the tiny love bite he gave me through my gown ignited my body like I was a bomb just waiting to explode. Thomar growled into my mouth, his struggle for control laughable with both Varin and I forcing our pleasure into his mind.

One thrust. Two. Thomar's body went rigid, his cock deep and hard, unforgiving. He gave me his seed and his soul together. I felt his complete surrender. There was no holding back, not for any of us. We would live or die together.

When it was over we remained in place, unmoving for long minutes, our heavy breathing the only sound in the small room.

Thomar kissed me gently, over and over, little love kisses that told me exactly how he cherished me. Adored me. Worshiped me.

Varin pulled the shoulder of my gown farther to the side so his lips could do the same to my shoulders, the back of my neck. His hands moved in slow, tender lines from my waist to my breasts over the soft fabric of my gown, the touch somehow more intimate through my clothing. More desperate.

I cried. The tears coming from somewhere deep within me, somewhere I'd hidden away and buried so long ago I'd forgotten they existed. *This* was what I had been longing for my entire life. Connection. Trust. Love.

So much love it was spilling from my eyes and my body. Their seed inside me felt like a pledge, a tribute. An oath.

"This is not the right time, but I cannot wait." Thomar sounded unsure, his lips moving to kiss a stray tear from the tip of my nose.

"Wait for what?"

"Varin?" he asked.

"Yes. By the gods, don't fucking wait."

Wait for what?

Thomar did not keep me in suspense. "Danika, do you accept me as your primary male? Do you trust me to love and protect you? Cherish you? Give you pleasure? Or do you with so choose another?"

Oh. My. God. The dream—matching simulation—from the testing center. This was what that warrior had said to his mate...*before* he'd fucked her brains out.

Leave it to my mates to break the rules. The thought made me smile. They were perfect. Absolutely perfect for me. "Yes, I accept your claim."

Varin's voice came at once, as if he'd been biting his tongue, forced to wait. "And do you accept me, Danika, as your second?"

"Yes. I accept you both. Of course I do." I leaned my forehead against Thomar's chest, uncaring that we were all still dressed, that my mates were in armor and that my gown was bunched up at my waist. "I love you. I love both of you. You better not die on me today."

The reminder of what we faced was a buzzkill, but we couldn't stay here forever, no matter how much I wanted to.

Thomar shuddered. "I will protect and care for you as long as I live."

"You honor us, Mate. You are ours now. We will honor and shield you. Keep you safe. No one will ever hurt you again."

I swallowed down tears at my mates' vows. I believed them and the relief flooding my body was unexpected and painful. I'd been on my own for so long. So damn long. This felt like a reprieve. A miracle. Thomar and Varin were my personal miracles.

Slowly, Varin pulled free of my body. I missed him at once, my pussy clamping down on Thomar's cock in protest of what I knew was coming.

Moments later I was on my feet, dressed once more. My mates had righted themselves and looked as if nothing had happened. Meanwhile, I knew I looked like I'd been crying.

"We must eat. Rest." Thomar looked at me and must have sensed my unease. He lifted me into his arms, cradled me to his chest so I could hide my face against his neck.

Varin moved to the door, opened it and checked the corridor beyond. "The corridor is empty." Varin looked at me. "Are you ready?"

"I need a couple more minutes."

Varin nodded and closed the door without question or complaint. Thomar took a seat with me in his lap. They were caring for me, helping me hide from the world. I needed a few minutes to find myself again. Maybe not to find myself. No. Remake myself now that I was theirs and they were mine. Until death do us part. There were no witnesses, no official ceremony. None of that mattered to me. Not now. Not when we were all dying.

Hopefully that wouldn't be in a few days for me. And if it were? I had no regrets. Still, it would be much better to save the prisoners, find that Nexus unit and make him tell us how to fix this mess.

Yes. That was a *much* better plan.

13

Thomar

The Hive prison ship appeared before our shuttle, looming in the pilot's view screen like a giant wall rushing toward us. With an expertise I admired, the Prillon warrior activated some kind of stealth technology I'd never seen before—another thing I would discuss with Helion later—and slipped our rescue team into an empty cargo bay without being detected. A second craft followed, this one a bit larger and capable of taking back any prisoners we managed to free.

I checked Danika's armor one more time. Varin had done an excellent job, the armor we'd adapted for our personal use fit her like a second skin. She had asked for a small weapon and Varin and I agreed she needed to be able to protect herself. He had crafted an ion blaster that fit her palm perfectly and a knife that would pierce Hive armor was strapped to her thigh. "Are you ready, mate?"

"Not really."

Had she lied to be or offered false bravado I would have forced her to remain on the shuttle. But my mate was fierce, protective and would undoubtedly follow me. Better to have her at our sides where we could protect her.

Varin leaned in close and kissed her temple. "We will protect you."

"I know. I trust you."

The truth of her statement made my heart ache. She spoke true. Other than Varin, no one had ever gifted me with such blind faith.

Unable to help myself, I kissed her once more before locking her helmet in place. When the shuttle door opened, Helion and his Atlan were first out the door.

We followed them into a large, deserted area of the ship. The abandoned section made me uneasy. Quiet. Covered in space dust and empty containers. It felt like a trap.

"According to our scans, the prisoners are on level four. The integration lab on level three and the hibernation chambers are on level five." Helion repeated the briefing we'd just had on the ship. We were all experienced warriors. There was no need.

"What level are we on?" Danika whispered to me.

"Six."

"Are there stairs?" She looked around the cargo bay and I felt her mind settle into the moment. Assessing risk. Looking for exits. She was not panicked or hysterical. Pride and sadness filled me at her reaction. She was strong. She'd had to be.

Perhaps that was why we understood each other so well. We fit. She was perfect for me in a way I had never dared imagine.

I would rip this entire ship to pieces to protect her if need be. Varin must have felt my determination as he turned to me and gave a slight nod. In my mind, his voice stirred.

Danika before all others.

Agreed.

In this we were of one mind. Danika was the single most important being on this ship. Her survival was paramount.

We moved out, Helion and his strike team clearing corridor after corridor as Governor Maxim, Ryston, Doctor Surnen, Varin and I took the rear, Rachel and Danika between our two groups.

We moved through the sixth floor with no enemy contact. The fifth made both Danika and Rachel gasp as we slipped past Hive who were asleep in their hibernation chambers.

"Can we save them, too? Wake them up or something?" Rachel asked Maxim.

Doctor Surnen shook his head. "Not while they are part of the collective mind."

Helion overheard and his voice came through the comms. "They will not be free until the Nexus unit is destroyed. Which is not our objective. Leave them."

Danika's irritation spiked and I felt her empathy for the warriors and fighters who had once been part of the Coalition Fleet.

We passed the last occupied chamber and I glanced

at a large Prillon warrior. His face and chest were bare and lined with scars. His legs were massive, clearly augmented with Hive tech. Attached to his wrists were specialized devices of some sort I'd never seen before.

Weapons, no doubt.

I moved past, turned to check behind us.

The Prillon stepped forward and turned to look at me.

Fuck. He had to be designated a Hive Soldier. They were larger than most, harder to kill.

"Get the females out of here. One of the Soldiers just woke up."

"Gods be damned. Move out," Helion ordered as I raised my rifle.

"No!" Danika raced to me, her hand coming down over my rifle. "Can't you feel him? He's fighting it."

Shocked by her words, I watched the Prillon as he sank to his knees. He lifted his hands to his head as if it were splitting in half. A feeling I knew well.

"Don't hurt him." Danika tried to walk past me but I blocked her with my arm until Varin could grab her from behind.

"Do not go near him." I was not in the mood for a debate.

Helion appeared at my side as I scanned the rest of the hibernation chambers for activity. There appeared to be none.

"Who are you?" Danika asked.

"We are---" He doubled over in pain, his forehead touching the cold floor. Seconds later he lifted his head and spoke to my female. "I am Bastion. Bastion Arcas of Prillon Prime."

I lowered my rifle. Fuck. My cousin? I had not seen the boy in two decades.

Clearly he was no longer a child, but a massive fucking Arcas warrior. And the Hive had integrated him, kept him here. Yet, he spoke to us as an individual. Knelt before us.

The agony in his gaze was one I recognized. "Cousin." I lifted my helmet to reveal my face. "I have not seen you since you were a child."

"Thomar? We thought you lost."

"I was." I turned my head to the side so Bastian could see the markings the Hive had left in my flesh. "Varin and I escaped."

Bastian shuddered, lowered his head to the floor. "I cannot look upon you. He will see you."

"The Nexus unit?" Danika asked.

"Yes."

"You are still fighting him." It was a statement, not a question. Danika's pride and warmth rolled through our collars. "You are truly an Arcas. Strong, like my mate, Thomar."

That had my cousin lift his head, but his eyes remained closed. "The females are on level two. The infants remain in the lab. Level three."

Helion protested. "Our scans indicate the female prisoners are on level three."

Bastion laughed, but there was no mirth in the sound. "A trap, Helion. The prison cells are not locked and they are full of Hive Soldiers."

"How many are guarding the females?" I asked.

"Do not know."

Damn. I believed him. "And the infants?"

"He will be there with his two. Dangerous."

"We outnumber them."

Bastion shook his head as if Helion were an idiot. "Your numbers are irrelevant."

"Why are you not with them?" Helion asked.

"We are too difficult to control." Bastian waved his arm around, indicating the other fifteen hibernation chambers. "We are a thorn in his side. We resist."

I knew of what he spoke. Varin and I had been the same, able to think despite the Hive influence. "Why didn't you leave? Escape from this prison?"

"The females." He groaned, clearly suffering. "Protect. The females."

"Oh my god. We can't leave them here either." Danika's compassion for my cousin and the others made my heart hurt. Varin pulled her to his side as I kept my weapon trained on my cousin. He was an Arcas. He was strong. But I knew he could lose control at any moment. I had been the same.

"You must," Bastion insisted. "I must sleep or he will —control." Bastion crawled back to his hibernation chamber and used the side walls to pull himself up to his full height. He leaned back, locking his head and neck into place. "Level two. You underestimate him."

"Who."

"Nexus Five." With those two words his eyes closed and his body became limp with sleep.

Danika took a step closer, her gaze lingering on the

tormented male. "Thomar?"

"Yes, love?"

"Look at his neck."

I moved closer and cursed. He wore a mating collar, but the item looked similar to Danika's, partially embedded in his flesh, merging with his mind and his body as hers was. As mine and Varin's had done. Varin stepped forward and inspected Bastion as well.

"Fuck." Varin looked at me. "Nothing we can do about it until we finish this. Level two first? Or three?"

Danika grabbed my wrist and tugged. I turned to face the only female I had ever loved. "The babies. He's with the babies. I can feel him."

As could I. I looked at Varin. He nodded.

"We will go to three, Helion. Take your team to two and free the females."

Governor Maxim cleared his throat from behind me. "We will go to level four and seal off the Hive Soldiers hiding in the prisoners' cells. Should buy us enough time to free the females and escape this ship."

"Agreed," I said.

Helion glared at me but I just raised a brow. He did not outrank me, as much as he wished it were so. I did not follow his orders, nor did I care what he desired. My mate needed to go to level three and face the Nexus unit. She would not rest until she saw the children freed with her own eyes. Her brother had suffered, and she had killed to protect him. She had not changed and would not go alone.

Maxim, Ryston, Doctor Surnen and Rachel moved away from us, back the way we had come. They would seal off level four. I was confident in their skills. They were mated now, but they had been warriors first.

I looked at Helion. "Well?"

"I'm coming with you." He turned to his team. "Go. Level three. Get the females. Meet us back at the shuttle. You have ten minutes."

The group moved out, all except Helion and one Atlan Warlord, the same one who seemed permanently attached to Helion's side. "Lead the way," Helion said to me.

I moved with some speed, careful that Danika could keep up. She did so, easily, her small ion blaster in her hand and ready to fire. I had the thought that she looked like a tiny, adorable thing with her tiny blaster. She lifted her gaze to mine.

"Don't you dare. I am *not* cute. I am scary and mean."

"Of course," I agreed. I was not a foolish male.

We reached the entrance to the integration lab on level three. With one glance at the others to ensure they were prepared, I opened the door.

We rushed into the room, fanned out, cleared the space.

Babies were crying. The sound heartbreaking and so very wrong in this space.

This empty, space.

"Where the fuck are they?" Varin asked.

Danika gasped and tilted her neck to look up. Way up. I felt them then. The enemy. Watching us. Hovering. Waiting to strike.

I lifted my gaze but it was too late, the Nexus unit was already on top of me.

14

Danika

The blue creature we had come here to find landed on top of Thomar and shoved him to the ground. I screamed as Varin went down under a huge Hive something—not blue, but Atlan big. Another dropped onto Helion.

Three tackled the Atlan Warlord who bellowed with rage and seemed to transform before my eyes. He got bigger and bigger, his face changing into a giant's, his hands huge.

A beast. He was turning into his beast.

Holy shit.

I shook, adrenaline making me frantic. I was the only one standing. Alone. Untouched.

"Scary and mean. Scary and mean." I chanted the words to myself as I lifted the small blaster Varin had made for me and pointed it at one of the three enemies stacked on top of the beast. They were thick and if I missed one, I'd most likely hit another.

I fired. One of the assailants went flying, blasted backward through the air to hit the wall.

The beast wasted no time flinging off a second. The third he grabbed in two huge hands and pulled.

The sound. Of squishing, tearing flesh made me gag and I turned away to find a new target.

Varin and Thomar were both frozen. Unmoving. Their gazes locked with their attackers.

Helion struggled, but he was not high on my list. And he was still moving.

Careful not to risk hitting Varin, I aimed at his attacker and fired.

The Hive shuddered. Blinked. His hold on Varin broken, my mate struck hard, sending the Hive to the floor. Varin pounced and I turned to Thomar.

It was not Thomar's gaze I found trained on me, waiting for me. It was the Nexus unit's black eyes. They were deep, an abyss that I tumbled into. I could not move. Could not think. I could only feel his need to connect. His barren, isolated existence. The endless acceptance and connection I would feel as part of him. One with him.

I wanted to belong. To be part of something. To be one.

No. That wasn't right. I wanted to be with Thomar and Varin. My mates. Not this thing. I didn't care how lonely he thought he was.

"Stop it. Get out of my head."

The Nexus unit smiled at me, his teeth a pale shade of icy blue. "At last, sister. You have come."

"I am not your sister." I raised the blaster and he raised his hands, palms out, as if he were surrendering and meant no harm. His fighters stopped moving as well. The Atlan had no mercy, ripping his remaining enemies into pieces. Helion blasted the one he'd been fighting with his weapon. Thomar and Varin seemed locked in place, frozen.

Helion shot and killed the enemy Varin had on the floor beneath him. One shot to the head.

Varin didn't move, his hands locked around the Hive Soldier's throat.

Why wasn't he moving?

"You are one of us. Do you not feel them? All of them are yours now." The Nexus lowered his jaw in a weird, inhuman manner and turned his attention to the infants in small cradle-like containers behind him. Not one was crying. They were quiet. Calm.

I could *feel them*. Their curious minds. Their hunger or thirst. If one was cool or too warm. Content or sleepy. There were five babies, all girls. Their tiny spirits seemed to latch on to me. As one, their small hands lifted into the air as if reaching for me. Calling to me.

What. The. Hell?

"What have you done to them?"

"Given them life."

"That's not what I mean." I sensed Helion and the beast moving behind me, but the Nexus seemed completely unconcerned, his focus remained on me. "Why can I feel them?"

"You are their mother. Their center. Their Nexus."

"No. I'm not. I'm dying. Whatever you did to me is killing me."

The Nexus pointed glanced down his nose at Thomar first, then Varin. My mates stirred in my mind, fighting the Nexus unit's control. They were close, close enough to rise and destroy him. Knowing they were with me again, I reached for them through our mating collars. *Not yet. I am fine. Not. Yet.*

Still ignoring Helion, the Nexus moved that black, heartless gaze to me. "You are three. You must survive."

"What are you talking about?"

The Nexus blinked and I was gone, out of my body, my mind his. I saw what he wanted me to see.

A war. Battleships. Fighting.

Not with the Prillons. Not with the Coalition ships. With someone else.

Something else. The things the Hive fought had no ships. No weapons I could see. They were darkness, moving darkness.

What are they? I asked, mind to mind.

The enemy.

I thought we were your enemy.

You are a resource that is nearly exhausted. We must adapt. With those words my vision switched to a medical setting. Multiple locations. Dozens of attempts to breed with Coalition females of all races. Their experiments were brutal. Cold. Clinical. And failures. Every single one.

Until now.

I staggered as he forced me to open my eyes and see the babies here, in this room.

"I don't understand."

He tilted his head as if irritated and my vision changed again. Once more I was in deep space, but this time the battle was huge, an entire solar system filled with explosions. Ships. Death.

The Hive were on one side, thousands of integrated fighters from the Coalition charging forward to fight an enemy I did not understand. Thousands of fighters fell. Destroyed. Every planet, rock and moon soaked in Coalition blood.

Angry, I pulled away from the vision. "Why don't you fight your own war?"

"We are few. You are many."

"Why didn't you ask for help?" I felt sorry for this thing now, and I hated that. I felt Thomar stirring in my mind, fighting his desire to protect me, forcing himself to remain still. The Nexus unit's focus was on me and not my mates. If Thomar decided to attack, the Nexus would have no time to escape.

The Nexus unit made a noise that sounded like an alarm of some kind. "We stood before Emperor Alamar Arcas and did as you suggest. We were refused."

Shock jolted through Thomar's body. Confusion. Thomar stood slowly, his hands up in a gesture that matched the blue creature's pose. Palms out. "That was hundreds of years ago."

"And has your answer changed, Arcas? You are here, killing my soldiers, ignoring our struggle. Still you deny the inevitable result of our failure."

"What failure?" Thomar asked.

"When we fall, you fall."

Wait. What? I was new to space but this entire conversation made no sense to me.

"I am not the emperor. Prillon Prime is not ruled by the Arcas family."

The Nexus tilted its head. "I smell your blood, royal. I see Alamar Arcas in your face."

"I speak the truth. An Arcas has not ruled Prillon Prime for hundreds of years."

"Interesting. I shall take this information back to the others." The Nexus unit literally disappeared into thin air.

"No!" Helion's shout filled empty space. "Gods be damned. He had a transport beacon. Fuck! Fuck! Fuck!" Helion kicked the table nearest him in a rage. "We needed him alive."

"Why?" I asked.

He ignored me—of course he did—and turned to the Atlan. "Let's get these babies out of here. Fuck. Gods be damned. This is a disaster."

The Altan lifted two babies, one in each hand. He held out one of the infants to Helion, who looked terrified and walked away. I lifted one of the baby girls into my arms and tried to remain calm as Varin took two more.

Thomar stood at the door, watching us. "I must retrieve Bastion. I cannot leave him here."

"Hurry." He disappeared with my blessing.

We carried the infants back to the original shuttle. I watched through the open doorway as the rest of our Colony crew raced toward us. Just beyond them, Helion's team escorted the women they'd found to the second, larger craft. One looked up and met my gaze. I was cradling the small girl I'd carried back to the shuttle. The vision of me holding the child seemed to calm her and she met my gaze, a clear question in her eyes.

I nodded and held up five fingers. Her shoulders sagged in relief and she boarded the craft.

"Let's get the fuck out of here." Ryston, Rachel's second, seemed particularly disturbed. Perhaps it was Rachel's reaction to the infants. She held both babies Varin had been carrying, tears streaming down her face.

"Not yet. Thomar is coming." I could feel him, his frustration. Urgency. I looked at Varin. "Is he being chased?"

Varin closed his eyes for a moment. Cursed. "Yes. Fuck." He kissed me on the top of my head and leaped from the shuttle. "I'll bring him back."

"Always. I know." I flooded him with love as he ran back into the prison ship and disappeared.

Moments later the cargo bay flooded with Hive fighters, their weapons firing at both shuttles.

"Guess they got out." Maxim's dry tone stated the obvious.

Helion dropped to the ground, his weapon firing. His Atlan bodyguard followed as he bellowed orders to his team on the other ship. "Get those females out of here. Now! Fucking move!"

His team literally lifted the remaining women off their feet, each warrior carrying a woman under each arm as they boarded the last few prisoners. One of the women smacked her warrior in the face, demanding to be put down.

He smiled at her and I nearly laughed. I knew that look. She'd just sealed her fate. That warrior was going to keep her.

The ship's doors were still closing when they took off. I breathed a sigh of relief when they were gone. The women were free now. No more torture. No more experiments.

"Come on, Thomar. Varin. Hurry." I rocked the baby in my arms and willed my mates to hurry.

Helion and the Warlord were being pushed back, closer to the shuttle. He shouted up at his pilot. "One more minute, then we go."

The pilot nodded and moved to take his seat in the cockpit. I blocked his path. "You leave my mates here and I will kill you myself."

He grinned at me and I knew he had no intention of following that particular order from Helion. Thank God. I looked back at the others and Maxim nodded his head at me. "He's mine. Colony pilot."

Rachel beamed up at him. "I knew there was a reason I loved you."

Maxim grinned at her, clearly smitten.

Ryston leaned down and whispered just loudly enough for all of us to hear. "We'll give you a few more reasons when we get home."

Rachel blushed. I did, too, thinking of all the various *reasons*—and positions—my mates gave me to love them.

The shuttle engines rumbled and I peeked out to see Thomar and Varin running, Bastion unconscious between them.

"Hurry. Hurry. Hurry."

A blaster of some kind hit Thomar in the back. A sting of pain bit me between my shoulder blades but Thomar didn't miss a step.

Helion and the Warlord moved out to meet them, firing into the Hive following them. As a group, the raced up the shuttle ramp. Maxim yelled for his pilot to take off and slammed his hand over the door. Ryston reached for Bastion, lifting the large Prillon from my mates' grasp and pulling him deeper into the shuttle.

The door closed and we were flying. Free. Alive.

For now.

I didn't breathe evenly until the pilot announced we were in open space with no sign of pursuit. My relief didn't last long.

"Governor, we have an issue."

Maxim stepped up to the cockpit. "What is it?"

"We're being ordered to reroute to Prillon Prime."

"By whom?"

"Prime Nial, sir."

"Fuck."

15

Danika, Prillon Prime

he shuttle landed in a massive stadium. The door opened and the ramp lowered but I did not move. Not yet. We'd been halfway here when the pilot informed Thomar and Varin that their presence, specifically, had been ordered. And mine.

Me? Ordered to show up by the king of the galaxy? King. Prime. Whatever. The whole thing was surreal. All I wanted to do was go back to The Colony, curl up in bed with my mates and ignore the rest of the world for a while.

Or, at least four days. After that?

I wasn't going to think about after.

We walked down the ramp, the rest of our shuttle crew behind us carrying the babies. I felt like I was stepping into a *Star Wars* movie. Thousands of Prillons, males, females and children, were seated in row upon row of spectator seats. We walked out of the shuttle onto a dirt pit like gladiators entering the fighting arena. And just like the movies about ancient Rome I'd seen on television, Thomar and Varin walked with me to face a raised dais where two huge Prillon warriors stood looking down on us. Between them stood a human woman. I realized that had to be Jessica, the new queen. The human who had been mated to an outcast with Hive integrations, outcasts, just like my mates.

She smiled down at me and I felt the icy lump in my chest melt a bit, just enough so that I felt like I could breathe.

Through the collars, I felt Thomar's unease and Varin's banked ire.

My mates did not trust this place, this ruler, or the Prillon citizens surrounding us. Their minds were prepared for battle. Ambush. Nothing good.

I tried to send them calm. Surely a woman from Earth, a member of the small human sisterhood out here in space, wouldn't smile at me like that if we were about to go to prison. Or have our throats slit.

A light breeze lifted the heat from my neck and bare shoulders. I was wearing a long, black gown with black ties. Black on black to match my collar. My mates' collars. Rachel explained to me about the Prillon families and their colors. She also told me that the Arcas family no longer had a color. Theirs had been taken away a long, long time ago by an emperor who didn't like Thomar's ancestor. Now they just wore black.

Irritated at the entire Prillon race, I'd used the S-Gen machine on the shuttle to make the blackest black dress ever created. Every stitch was black. I pulled my hair up into a black clip and generated long black gloves that covered my arms nearly to my shoulders. I felt like a princess from a fairy tale. Except for my boots. They had small heels, but they were black, black steel in the tips— just in case. And my dress? Slit all the way to my hip on both sides, the little blaster Varin had given me strapped to my thigh. If Thomar and Varin were worried, I was going to be ready for anything.

Apparently, this ancestor had gone crazy and killed his own mate. Since the Arcas family was known for hot tempers and killer instincts on the battlefield, their entire family suffered from that disgrace. On the trip here, Thomar had filled me in on any missing bits of the story. He'd also explained that harming a female, any female, was the worst thing a Prillon male could do.

Killing one's own mate? Unthinkable.

I didn't care what this Prime or his idiots in the crowd thought of my mates. I knew the truth of them. They were honorable. Strong. Loving. Protective. Obsessive.

Perfection.

And they were mine.

Or were they? I'd heard about this queen, Jessica, and how she'd let her mates claim her in front of an entire arena of people.

I looked around. Perhaps *this* arena.

"Stay close to me," Thomar instructed, his body moving to stand between me and the Prillon guards nearest him on the left side of the dais.

"Do not fear, mate." Varin took up a similar position

on my other side, his hand resting on business end of the modified rifle still strapped to his back.

Thomar wore his as well, but his hands were at his sides as he stepped toward the king—ruler—Prime. Whatever. I didn't care who this guy was. I wanted to get my mates back to our room on The Colony and get them naked so I could check every single inch of their skin for injuries, wave the magic green wand over them and then make them fill me up with both of their cocks at once. I didn't want to worry about politics or the future. I wanted every minute I had left to be about pleasure. Love.

Remind these remarkable males that they were mine. That's what I wanted. I wanted to claim *them* and patience was not one of my virtues. Especially now, after seeing them in their element. Fighting. Protecting others. Their bravery and discipline when we faced that Nexus unit had blown my mind. The way they had gone back for Bastion. They were more than warriors, they were superheroes.

The crowd was restless as we walked across the grounds. When we stood still at last, Prime Nial raised his hand and the crowd went silent. "People of Prillon Prime. Today we honor two warriors worthy of the title."

The crowd roared for a few moments. Thomar and Varin darted a glance at one another, utterly confused.

I grinned and caught Jessica's eye. She winked at me.

Oh, yes. This was going to be good.

"Prince Thomar Arcas, members of the Arcas family, please make yourself known to me."

Thomar stepped forward as scattered members of the

crowd stood to be acknowledged. I glanced at each one briefly, curious about Thomar's family.

The males were big. As big as Thomar. Their faces grim. The females stood stiffly and I understood what they must be feeling. If their mates, fathers and brothers were anything like Thomar, they didn't deserve the way they'd been treated their whole lives any more than my mate did.

Prime Nial raised his hand again and the crowd went silent. I glanced to over my shoulder and realized several huge screens were displaying the entire thing. I looked about three times my normal height on that thing and I wondered who could see it? Just the people here? Did they have broadcast television?

"Prince Thomar Arcas, you battled in the Hive wars for fifteen years. You were captured with your second, Varin Mordin, and fought the mind control of a Nexus unit to escape. You suffered agony unlike any other warrior but found the courage to accept an Interstellar Bride. You returned to a Hive prison ship and freed twenty-seven female captives and five infants. You stand before me now, after a lifetime of dishonor and distrust from your own people with your head high, your mate and your second at your side.

Let it be known that from this day forward, the Arcas name is honored once more. The royal bloodline of Arcas is welcome in the arena. Prince Thomar Arcas, I restore your title, your privilege and your honor to you and your family."

The crowd seemed frozen for a few seconds. Shocked? I swallowed hard and waited.

What were they waiting for?

I glanced into the crowd and saw several of Thomar's family members touching their throats, violet bands were black had been moments ago.

His family color was violet? Like rainbow beautiful, rare violet?

Nice.

The spectators seemed to heave a collective breath and...scream. The noise was deafening and went on for long minutes. In my mind, Thomar's relief was quiet. Reserved.

He turned and looked at me. He didn't care about this ceremony.

He cared about getting me naked, his desire rushing through my mind. His hard cock on display for my appreciation.

Next to me, Varin chuckled. "One track mind."

Prime Nial rose his hand again and motioned Varin forward. He stepped up next to Thomar and stood, hands clasped behind his back as if he hadn't a care in the world.

He didn't care about this either. They had made their choices years ago. Lived with the consequences. Were at peace with their decisions.

As was I. Volunteering to be a bride was the best thing that I had ever done. These two, my mates, a miracle didn't expect. I was grateful for whatever time we had left.

"Captain Varin Mordin, your family disavowed you when you chose to fight with Thomar Arcas. You persisted. You have battled next to him, honored him, served as his second and protected your female with honor."

The crowd cheered again, but Prime Nial hushed them. "I ask you both now to serve on my war council."

This shocked both of my mates. I smiled. Finally, something was ruffling their feathers.

The queen, Jessica, stepped forward. She had a little girl on her hip. Adorable. Smiling. Maybe two years old. "Lady Arcas, I would ask you to remain on Prillon Prime as well. I would add you to the Queen's council and ask that you oversee the care and healing of the women from Earth that must now, remain here."

Me? What? "I'm not a psychologist. They are going to need therapy." Not that I wanted to refuse a queen, but these women needed more than I could give them.

"You will have all the resources you require. And you understand what they have suffered. You have suffered. You have endured imprisonment. You are from their home world. They need an advocate like you."

Well, when she put it that way. "I accept, on one condition."

She grinned at me. "And what is your condition?"

I looked around the arena, spotted a large chair, kind of like a throne near the center of the arena. If Jessica could do it, I could. Rachel said it was the highest honor a bride had ever given her Prillon mates. I wanted that for my mates. They were honorable. Good. Their people needed to know that I believed that with every cell in my body. "I ask that my mates be allowed to claim me here. Now. And that all here would serve as witness."

Thomar dropped his weapon.

Varin staggered like a drunken man.

I smiled, lifted the gown off over my head and walked naked to the throne in the center of the stadium.

Varin

BY THE GODS. This could not be happening.

Thomar watched our mate walk to the center of the arena. His cock as hard as mine, no doubt, his heart breaking.

No. Do not deny her. Do not.

Thomar spoke, his heartbreak in his voice. "My queen, I am honored by my mate's request. But I must inform all here that she is braver than any warrior. More giving and compassionate than you can imagine. She offers us this prize with no thought for herself. She is dying, my queen. As are we."

The Prillons in attendance hushed as if we had stolen their tongues.

"Explain."

"The Hive used all three of us for an experimental type of integration. Their implants cannot be removed and they are poison in our bodies. Danika has but a few days to live."

The queen gasped, her gaze locked on Danika's retreating back. "Then I suggest you do not make her wait."

I grinned, eager to make our claim official, make

Danika ours. Honor her in front of the Prime, our queen, and the entire planet.

"Not so fast, you two." Doctor Surnen stepped forward, Helion next to him. And standing next to Helion was Bastion Arcas.

"Bastion?" Thomar's shock was obvious.

"Bastion Arcas, like his cousin, was taken and integrated with the same technology. However, we have discovered a dampening device within his system that can be copied and implanted in you, Prince Arcas, as well as into your second and your mate."

My heart skipped a beat. Two.

"How long will we live, doctor? With this new implant?"

Doctor Surnen smiled. Even Helion looked pleased. "You will have a full, normal life. Perhaps longer. We do not fully understand the implants yet."

Thomar took a moment to process this news. I was done waiting. Walking across the arena to our mate, I disrobed as I did so, dropping a piece of armor every couple of steps. The crowd cheered me on with each piece that landed in the dirt. "Thomar?"

My shout moved him and he followed me, the Prillons going wild.

I was kissing Danika, her soft skin under my palms, her body melting into mine as Thomar approached. We would be truly one now. No death. No horror awaiting us. A lifetime of sacrifice and struggle rewarded with this, our mate. Thousands of our people cheering. A place at Prime Nial's side.

We would have to discuss what Danika had learned

from the Nexus unit. But not now.

Now was for fucking. Filling her. Making her whimper and moan and beg for more.

Now was for loving the female who had saved us both.

—————

Thomar

NONE of this should have mattered to me. I had grown hard, my heart stone. Until her.

She lifted her arms as I approached, Varin already in place, seated in the chair, ready to fuck her ass as I filled her pussy. We were all naked. Bared to the entire Coalition of planets. I knew this was being broadcast to every ship and planet. Every shuttle and canteen.

None had been honored in this way, not in hundreds of years, except Prime Nial and his second, Ander.

And now, us.

My family remained standing, their violet collars sparkling and brilliant in the light. My eyes filled with tears and I buried them in Danika's hair to hide them whose who did not deserve to see them.

They were for her. Her. Varin. Me. My family.

I kissed her, hard, as Varin slid deep into her ass. She moaned in welcome, her arms wrapped around my neck, pulling me down to her. The crowd disappeared as I slipped my fingers into her wet pussy. She was ready. More than ready.

"I love you. Both of you. I love you."

I kissed her ear. The place above her heart. As Varin struggled to remain still, I raised my voice so all could hear.

"Do you accept my claim, mate? Do you give yourself freely to me and my second? Or do you wish to choose another primary male?" My voice carried. The crowd hushed to hear Danika's response.

"I accept your claim, warriors. I love you."

My chest nearly exploded at her added words. She did not need to declare love for us, only that she believed we would protect and care for her. She honored us with her words. "Then we claim you in the rite of naming. You are mine and I shall kill anyone who dares harm you."

Varin spoke as well. "You are mine, Danika. I shall fight, die and live for no other but you."

The Prillons heaved a collective sigh. "May the gods witness and protect you." Their chant was still in my ears as I looked into Danika's eyes and slid deep.

She welcomed us. Accepted us, scars, imperfections. Our past. Our mistakes.

We moved. Fucked her. Gave her pleasure, as was our duty and our right.

For the first time in my life, I was finally home.

———

THANK you for reading Claimed by the Cyborgs. I hope you enjoyed it. Have you read my new DRAGON shifter book? Check it out!

Dragon Chains

Dragon shifters, fake identities, and betrayal; secrets that will either turn two strangers into bitter enemies or forge a passionate, burning love with the strength to last an eternity...

SENT HALFWAY across the world in her identical twin sister's place to sign a contract with a reclusive billionaire, Katy Toure has no idea what she's walking into. Before she signs anything, however, she meets the most amazing, drop-dead gorgeous man of her dreams. Even if all she can have with him is one night, she can't resist the hunger in his eyes or the way he makes her body sing.

Ryker Draquonir, king of the dragon shifters, takes one look at the woman sent to sign a contract with him, a contemporary marriage of convenience, and knows she is an impostor. Fate has stepped in after centuries on his own to give him his heart's desire; for the woman standing before him is his true mate.

Ancient Draquonir law forbids Ryker from revealing the existence of dragons and other magical creatures to her before he has claimed her, so if he wants a chance at happily ever after, he will have to seduce her to get it; woo her as only a billionaire can. Dragons love to hunt, and he will do anything to capture his true mate's heart.

Dragon Chains

A SPECIAL THANK YOU TO MY READERS...

Want more? I've got **hidden** bonus content on my web site *exclusively* for those on my <u>mailing list.</u>

If you are already on my email list, you don't need to do a thing! Simply scroll to the bottom of my newsletter emails and click on the ***super-secret*** link.

Not a member? What are you waiting for? In addition to ALL of my bonus content (great new stuff will be added regularly) you will be the first to hear about my newest release the second it hits the stores—AND you will get a free book as a special welcome gift.

Sign up now! http://freescifiromance.com

FIND YOUR INTERSTELLAR MATCH!

YOUR mate is out there. Take the test today and discover your perfect match. Are you ready for a sexy alien mate (or two)?

VOLUNTEER NOW!

interstellarbridesprogram.com

DO YOU LOVE AUDIOBOOKS?

Grace Goodwin's books are now available as audiobooks...everywhere.

LET'S TALK!

Interested in joining my **Sci-Fi Squad**? Meet new like-minded sci-fi romance fanatics and chat with Grace! Get excerpts, cover reveals and sneak peeks before anyone else. Be part of a private Facebook group that shares pictures and fun news! Join here:

https://www.facebook.com/groups/scifisquad/

Want to talk about Grace Goodwin books with others? Join the **SPOILER ROOM** and spoil away! Your GG BFFs are waiting! (And so is Grace) Join here:

https://www.facebook.com/groups/ggspoilerroom/

GET A FREE BOOK!

JOIN MY MAILING LIST TO BE THE FIRST TO KNOW OF NEW RELEASES, FREE BOOKS, SPECIAL PRICES AND OTHER AUTHOR GIVEAWAYS.

http://freescifiromance.com

ALSO BY GRACE GOODWIN

The Virgins - Complete Boxed Set

Interstellar Brides® Program: Ascension Saga

Ascension Saga, book 1

Ascension Saga, book 2

Ascension Saga, book 3

Trinity: Ascension Saga - Volume 1

Ascension Saga, book 4

Ascension Saga, book 5

Ascension Saga, book 6

Faith: Ascension Saga - Volume 2

Ascension Saga, book 7

Ascension Saga, book 8

Ascension Saga, book 9

Destiny: Ascension Saga - Volume 3

Interstellar Brides® Program: The Beasts

Bachelor Beast

Maid for the Beast

Beauty and the Beast

The Beasts Boxed Set

Starfighter Training Academy

The First Starfighter

Starfighter Command

Elite Starfighter

Starfighter Boxed Set

Other Books

Dragon Chains

Their Conquered Bride

Wild Wolf Claiming: A Howl's Romance

ABOUT GRACE

Grace Goodwin is a USA Today and international best-selling author of Sci-Fi and Paranormal romance with over a million books sold. Grace's titles are available worldwide on all retailers, in multiple languages, and in ebook, print, audio and other reading App formats.

Grace is a full-time writer whose earliest movie memories are of Luke Skywalker, Han Solo, and real, working light sabers. (Still waiting for Santa to come through on that one.) Now Grace writes sexy-as-hell sci-fi romance six days a week. In her spare time, she reads, watches campy sci-fi and enjoys spending time with family and friends. No matter where she is, there is always a part of her dreaming up new worlds and exciting characters for her next book.

Grace loves to chat with readers and can frequently be found lurking in her Facebook groups. Interested in joining her **Sci-Fi Squad**? Meet new like-minded sci-fi romance fanatics and chat with Grace! Get excerpts, cover reveals and sneak peeks before anyone else. Join here: https://www.facebook.com/groups/scifisquad/

Want to talk about Grace Goodwin books with others? Join the **SPOILER ROOM** and spoil away! Your GG BFFs are waiting! (And so is Grace) Join here:

https://www.facebook.com/groups/ggspoilerroom/

Printed in Great Britain
by Amazon